ELEMENTS OF HORROR: HORROR: Book One EARTH

DISCLAIMER: "This is a work of fiction. Names, characters, places and incidents are products of the author's imagination and are used fictitiously. Any resemblance to actual events, locales or persons, living or dead, is entirely coincidental."

Cover Design by Red Cape Graphic Design

Www.redcapepublishing.com/red-cape-graphic-design

Foreword

Welcome to Book One: Earth, the first in a series of four anthologies based on the Elements. Within these pages you will find a variety of stories from some of the best independent horror writers on the scene today. We hope you enjoy the deliciously dark tales, and that you will go on to read more by the authors involved in this book. Keep an eye out for the rest of series, all due for release in the later part of 2019.

Coming soon;

Book Two: Air
Book Three: Fire
Book Four: Water

Table of Contents

Pro-Death

Theresa Jacobs

Desperate, the girl lying upon the hard bed grabbed the white-gloved hand. "Please," she pleaded, "don't destroy my baby." Her eyes, limpid pools, released tears that coursed across her temples and into her hair.

"Shh." The nurse leaned in quick, as though she was going to plant a tender kiss on the eighteen-year-old's forehead; instead, her lips brushed the teen's ear. "I'll do what I can." The girl's hand squeezed harder, whether in thanks or for added reassurance, the nurse couldn't discover as she pulled back when Doctor Fairbanks approached.

Without acknowledging the youth on his table, or his employee, he dropped onto his stool and rolled the steel tray laden with medical scissors, forceps, needles, and other terrifying looking instruments, closer. "Did she take the Vicodin?" he asked, inspecting a fat syringe with a long, wide tube at the tip.

"Yes, Doctor."

The girl's cheeks reddened at the way she was being treated. She had to bite her lip to keep from bawling. She didn't want to give him the satisfaction of seeing her reactions.

Ten minutes later, Doctor Fairbanks snapped off his gloves, his lips twisted, an ugly snarl of disdain riding his handsome face. "I will not see you again," he said and left the room.

The nurse pretended to be busy and unaware of the scene playing out before her. The staff knew he misled pretty young girls often, but they kept a blind eye to save their jobs. When the door clicked shut, she spun and pressed the small white bag between the girl's breasts. "I could lose my job for this," she said, her brow raised, "you understand?"

The girl clutched the paper bag. It was no bigger than her last allergy prescription refill. She felt the hard-plastic bottle inside. Was it warm, or was it her imagination? Unable to speak, she closed her eyes, nodding yes, she did understand. When she opened them again, she was alone; the nurse had abandoned her too.

She slid from the table. The paper gown crinkled with every move and she ripped it off, no longer wanting to feel vulnerable. The chilled air of the stark office touched her skin for the briefest of moments before she tore back into her own clothes. They rode askew on her cold body, but she didn't care. Now was not the time for vanity.

The anguish rose again as she entered the waiting room where numerous other women of varying ages waited to abort their babies. She crammed the bag under the protection of her fall jacket and bolted from the room. She wanted to scream at them, *he's a monster, a killer, a user, run - all of you run!* Instead it was only her that ran.

She leapt down the concrete steps two at a time. If she fell and broke her own neck, she'd be happy. But death did not call on her today, it only visited and left a gaping wound.

As if to match her mood, the clouds imparted their sorrow, tears from the heavens above rained upon her. Without premeditated thought, or at least she didn't think it was a conscious choice, she ran across the tail end of the golf course, through a copse of trees and directly into the cemetery. Headstone after headstone a familiar comfort. Most she knew by size, or epitaph, or sad winged angel forever resting with the soul beneath. The saddest one of all, her mother's, beckoned her. She skidded before it and fell to her knees.

"I'm sorry. I'm sorry!" she wailed, her tears now flooding with the rain. She was no longer breathing but gasping great sobbing heaves. Bringing the small crushed bag out from under her arm, she pressed it to her cheek. She wanted to look. To see her baby. Would it have formed fingers and toes? Would it look like anything other than a tiny tadpole? Tilting her head back she screamed into the sky.

Hiccups over-rode her crying and she knew what must be done. She kissed the sodden bag. "I loved you before I knew you and I'll love you until I meet you."

The rain poured in long heavy drops, she was soaked to the bone and didn't care. Taking the top of the bag in her mouth, she wouldn't dare set her child down, not yet. She dug her fingers into the thick grass at the base of her mother's tombstone. Her nails scraped the granite stone, ripping them to the quick. Her blood mixed with the mud as she dug deeper. Able to get a handful of dirt, followed by another, she felt the hole was deep enough, and pressed the white bag into place. The safest of all. With her mom, who would cradle her grandchild until the end of time.

"Tabby?"

The voice floated hollow and meaningless through the storm-laden afternoon, as she re-covered the hole and her lost baby. Her body found more tears of shame and sorrow. She smeared her own face with muck as she hid behind her hands.

"Tabby! Come child, you're going to catch a death." The old woman, cozied in an oversized yellow slicker and black galoshes walked up to the girl, wrapping a similar jacket across her shoulders.

Tabatha closed her eyes and let her grandmother lead her away.

***

No words were spoken until they'd shucked their gear in the small porch. "I'm going to draw you a nice hot bubble bath and make you a tincture to forget your pain," Grandma said, hanging their coats to dry.

Tabatha said nothing, only stood comatose and motionless. There were no tears left, no feeling, no thought. She was an empty shell of flesh, bone, blood, and nerves, nothing more.

The old woman left her there for a moment. She hurried into the kitchen, plucking valerian, willow bark, ginger, and winter mint, boiled the kettle, and added a touch of belladonna to her purpose. Less than five minutes later she led her granddaughter to the bathroom where she started the bath to warm, placed a few drops of Argan oil to the steamy water, before pouring in some rose-scented bubble-bath. The wise woman knew the girl would not want to glance upon her own naked body for some time, and slowly undressed her, before aiding her into the water.

Tabatha moved by rote, but responded to nothing; not her grandmother, not the water, not even being disrobed like a child.

Once her grandchild was sunk up to her neck in bubbles, she handed Tabatha the hot mug. "Sip it, my child," she cooed. "This will help you relax, ease your discomfort, and help you forget."

Tabatha's red-rimmed eyes came into focus, taking in her grandmother's deep brown ones. "I don't want to forget," she breathed, barely a whisper. Her grandmother reached forward, in her one hand she held a paring knife, in the other a small glass bowl. Tabatha watched unmoving, or questioning, as she scraped dirt from under the nails that weren't split to the flesh.

"What's his name?"

"Morgan Fairbank. Doctor Morgan Fairbank," Tabatha said, a single tear finding its way out of her dehydrated body.

Her grandma clucked her tongue. "The father and the...?" She didn't need to finish.

Tabatha nodded, sniffed and gulped down the rest of her tea. "Can I sleep now?"

"Yes, my sweet. You sleep, I'll keep watch."

Tabatha's eyes closed, her head lolled against the back of the deep tub while her grandmother hunkered down on the floor to work. She spit into the bowl of what little dirt she'd gathered and began kneading the muck with her fingers. Reaching up, she dipped her sleeping grandchild's fingers into the water. When she pulled them back up, she let a few drops of bath water, pink with blood, mix into her concoction. The room grew foggy with steam and grandma began to chant her spell.

***

"What the hell?" Glimpsing his house through the barren trees, Morgan let his foot off the gas. He squinted, trying to get a better visual as anger bubbled in his chest. He sped up to only slam on his brakes twenty seconds later. He jammed the shifter into park and flung open the car door. Every light in his glass-walled forest designer home was ablaze. Even from where he stood in the driveway, he could see furniture toppled over and items in disarray.

His heart raced as he ran up the stone path to the front door. It was left ajar and dry brittle leaves had found their way into the open concept home; for he resided an hour outside of town and it had not yet rained.

"SARA!" Morgan called out, his eyes trying to take in what had happened. Were they burgled? It made no sense, they lived in the middle of nowhere. "SAR..." his voice caught in his throat as he noticed the fuchsia lipstick, Sara's favorite color, in the form of a letter scribbled across his 80-inch television screen.

His mouth gaped as he read.

YOU FUCKING BASTARD YOU WERE WITH ANOTHER WHORE AGAIN LAST ONE I WARNED YOU NOW BE PREPARED FOR MY WRATH

He spun, taking in the destruction of his million-dollar home. Every drawer was open, the contents dumped or tossed about, the couch cushions scattered, kicked to various corners. Chairs upended, and the ornate pieces that gave the home color, strewn about the floor, for no apparent reason, other than perhaps in a fit of rage Sara was aiming to hurt something.

"Son of a bitch!" he yelled at the mess around him and kicked a tipped over lamp putting an added dent in the already dented shade. "Idiot," he berated himself, "no more wives. Just fuck the sluts and move on."

He righted a chair and picked up a decorative silver spiral-thingy setting it back onto the coffee table, but there was too much mess, too much to do. Running his hands through his hair he sighed. "Screw it," he said. Resigned to dealing with the mess later, or not doing it at all and calling in a cleaning crew, Morgan pressed the button on the wall to shut off the main floor lights. He no longer wanted to see the chaos and felt a sudden desire to go check his safe, see if she left him anything.

Darkness engulfed him and he paused as a gust of wind howled through the trees cracking the dry branches together like stiletto heels on stone. For the briefest moment he thought Sara was walking up the path, and his heart raced again; he was ready to fight. But then a greater gust came and the leaves in the foyer whipped up into a whirlwind, snapping him back to reality.

"Ah shit." He hurried back through the wide living space to close the front door against the coming storm. Morgan was looking forward to it. He enjoyed sitting in his glass study with a 150-year-old cognac and cigar, (which all his ex-wives detested), and watching the world get beaten by the weather. Tonight, things would be no different, in spite of his soon to be sixth ex-wife.

The leaves lifted in unison, rising above him. Startled, he stopped and gasped. They appeared to pause as if thinking before crashing down upon him like an errant wave at the beach. Morgan covered his eyes against the onslaught of piercing dry edges and scratching stems. "Jesus Christ." He flailed at the battering leaves and shielded his eyes to get the door closed and put an end the madness.

The wind gusted harder. It echoed through his house, calling

Moooorrrrgggaaan, along the way. Tiny specks of dirt followed. Morgan tripped back a step, the leaves a frenzy around his head. No matter how much he swatted, grasped, or danced, they did not relent. Grains of dust tickled his sinuses, causing him to sneeze. They came faster and harder, and fuller, entire clods of dirt pelted him.

"What's happening?" He coughed, falling to his knees amidst a savage dirt devil.

The light from the kitchen faded to dim as the earth filled the room. Debris comprised of soil, pine needles, twigs, a variety of leaves, and shed animal fur and droppings, hurtled into every open room, battering all surfaces. Stones, heavier than the wind would normally move, came flying into his house. They pinged off his glass walls, leaving small puckers in the panes. He cried out as a rock knocked against his head. The earth spun around him and specks tore at his flesh, stinging and slicing. Desperate to get out the path of destruction, Morgan hunkered into himself and began to half-slide, half-crawl towards the back of the house where his bathroom lay.

The sheer volume of dust and debris grew within seconds, forming a volatile tornado inside his home. The wind became a cacophony of colliding terra firma. Morgan was engulfed by it. His hair flew about his head. No longer able to move, but only tuck his face into his arms to protect himself, the earth beat him raw.

A gunshot crack reverberated through the forest. Inside his own personal hell, Morgan did not hear it. The lamp he kicked earlier slid across the floor, knocking into his foot. That crack he did hear as his ankle snapped. He screamed into his sleeve at the instant pain, while his mind was screaming, *STOP!* Yet he dared not open his mouth or he'd choke on the dirt that hammered him.

Another crack sounded, this time shaking the house on its foundation. Morgan felt it through the floor. *Oh god, now what? What else can go wrong? Help. I need help.* He moaned through the torture; doing something he hadn't done since he was a boy, he began to call on God.

When the next crack came, he didn't have time to think, pray, or scream, as a forty-foot pine fell through his glass house, shattering windows and imploding the roof. The heavy trunk landed across the supine doctor, crushing him to a pulp. The roots danced in the night air and moist earth rained down to the needle-carpeted ground. The wind died in that instant. The whirlwind slowed, releasing the captive forest floor and it rained upon the shattered glass house.

***

Tabatha awoke knowing she'd done the right thing letting Morgan abort their baby. It didn't ease her pain, but it did give her a new understanding of what she wanted for her future. She would find a good man who would love her, not just her body, and together they would have a family. It was time to focus on the next steps in her life, to make a career and become a real woman. Her hands still moved to her belly, but thanks to her grandmother there was no physical pain. As for her heart, that'd take a little longer to heal.

Tabatha's cheeks reddened with shame as she found her grandmother already sitting at the kitchen table. Sun streamed through the kitchen windows. The night's storm has cleared to create a stunning, perfect fall day, that in no way matched her mood.

"Morning, gran," she said, keeping her eyes focused on getting a bowl from the cupboard and pouring in cereal, followed by cold milk.

"Lovey, you're looking better today," Grandma replied and clicked on the small kitchen TV.

Tabatha sat beside her and gave her cheek a dry kiss. "I don't know what I'd do without you, gran. About last night..."

Her grandmother smiled and pointed at the TV. "Breaking news" flashed across the screen.

Tabatha's attention was drawn away from the events of yesterday and into the world today.

The newscaster, a gorgeous woman about thirty years old, stood in the forest, the backdrop a pile of rubble covered in black glass and downed trees.

"At 6:00 am this morning, Sara Fairbank, the wife of the controversial abortion doctor Morgan Fairbank, called 911 to report their state-of-the-art home had been destroyed. As you can see behind me, there appear to be eight large trees down around the once-stunning glass home of the Fairbanks. Currently the authorities don't know what caused so many trees to seemingly uproot themselves from the ground. The largest tree," the reporter turned to move out of the camera's view and show the root ball that appeared to be as tall as a house, hovering outside of the shattered home. "A large pine, fell directly onto the home, crushing it. At this moment, Mrs. Fairbank has not been able to reach Doctor Fairbank and has no inclination of his whereabouts. Emergency crews are working as quickly as possible to clear some of the debris in the event that the doctor is trapped inside the home. We'll have an update on the noon report and again at six. Thanks for watching, I'm...."

Tabatha's mouth fell open and milk dribbled down her chin. She stopped listening and looked at her grandmother wide-eyed. "Did you?" Her spoon aimed at the screen, which now panned to a not-distraught looking Sara Fairbank, who sat in her Porsche talking on her cell phone.

Grandma winked and said, "Eat your breakfast, dear, we have errands to do today."

The End

Beneath the City

Jaq D. Hawkins

"I don't know which I'm more scared of, getting caught on CCTV and arrested, or getting electrocuted. Jonathan, this is a really stupid idea!" Kyle looked over his shoulder at the diminishing light of the London underground tunnel, then with a quick glance at his two companions, he continued watching his feet to be sure he didn't touch the center rail.

"It's more likely we'll get hit by a train before then." Nicola gave Kyle a wicked grin. If Jonathan hadn't involved her in this insane adventure, Kyle never would have agreed to come. It didn't take psychic powers to know that was exactly why Jonathan had done it.

"Just think," Jonathan pointed out with a smirk. "If you hadn't been too scared to go dancing with us last night, we'd have a massive hangover now and we wouldn't have come here today!"

"You know I'm too self-conscious to dance in public!" Kyle touched the wall with his fingertips, trying as best he could to orient himself in the diminishing light.

"Says the guy who jumps out of perfectly good airplanes and calls it fun!" Jonathan teased.

"So, I like to skydive!" Kyle strained to see the reflection of light on the tracks. His mouth was getting dry and thoughts of turning back warred with the timing of the next train that Jonathan had predicted. "At least it's in the open. I don't like these walls closing in on me. How much farther is this fissure you said you saw?"

"Just up here." Jonathan turned on the inadequate pen light he had brought. "A few more steps."

Kyle could only see his friends as shadow silhouettes now. They had all dressed in their darkest clothing, which meant jeans that weren't too badly faded and band T-shirts for himself and Jonathan. Nicola was still easy to differentiate in the dark because of her shoulder-length hair, dark auburn in the light, and a little pale skin from her midriff beneath the black crop top that had helped convince Kyle that exploring dark places in her company wasn't out of the question.

He wished he had ignored Jonathan's cautions about getting caught and had brought a better light with them. Kyle listened closely for sounds of a train. Nicola was right. The danger of getting hit by one was astronomical, although he presumed workmen must have to hug the walls sometimes.

"Here it is!" Jonathan called back, his excitement palpable.

Despite his fears, Kyle couldn't help sharing in some of Jonathan's elation, though it might have been mostly relief at getting off the tracks.

Kyle caught up with his friend and followed the beam of light tracing the jagged, narrow pyramid-shaped opening in the cement wall. The passage beyond was pitch black.

"Listen!" Nicola hissed. Both boys stayed silent a moment, straining their ears to identify a rhythmic sound, barely detectable in the stillness.

"Is it a train?" Kyle whispered.

"Get inside!" Nicola urged them. Nobody argued.

Without any need to say it aloud, all of them stayed quiet, listening. The rhythm continued, unchanging. After a few moments, Kyle broke the silence.

"If it's a train, it's not moving anywhere."

"That's what I was telling you," Jonathan explained. "The power cut made the train stop here and nothing was moving, but that steady beat kept on. That was when I cupped my hands on the window and saw the fissure. I figured the sound was coming from there."

Kyle shot a sceptical glance in his friend's direction, though no one could see his expression in the darkness.

"Look!" Jonathan turned something on the pen light and the narrow beam widened to illuminate the expanse of the walls.

Nicola's breath caught.

"It's so pretty!"

Jonathan moved the light slowly over the enclosing rock while they all took in the glitter of reflective stone scattered across the surface.

"Gemstones?" Kyle asked.

"Maybe just quartz." Nicola had applied to university to study geology. "But the way it sparkles! It's amazing!"

Kyle had to agree, though he only nodded his head before it occurred to him that his friends might not see the gesture if the light wasn't directed at him.

Jonathan moved the beam to look down what looked like a corridor cut through solid rock. The pulse of sound seemed to be emanating from that direction. He walked forward slowly, closely followed by the others huddling towards the light.

A turn in the path brought them to an opening on the left, unmistakeably the work of an intentional hand. It was an almost perfect rectangle, slightly wider at the bottom, leading to a separate path. The rhythm came louder from that direction.

"We've gone far enough," Kyle pleaded. "We could get lost down here..."

"Do you think the people who dug the underground made these tunnels?" Jonathan asked, ignoring Kyle's attempt at common sense.

"But why?" Nicola speculated aloud. "Look!"

She pointed down the new tunnel and Jonathan turned the penlight, revealing a series of similar openings branching off both sides of the tunnel. The sparkling rocks covered much of the walls, making good use of the feeble light.

"Oh man," Jonathan acknowledged. "You're right about getting lost. It's like an underground warren."

"I wonder if it's mapped in any of the city records?" Nicola stepped forward, straining to see down the new passages without veering off the central path.

Kyle followed her, gingerly stepping slowly as if some instinct impelled him to stay as quiet as possible.

"I've never heard of anything like this. You would think rumours would get around if anyone knew..."

"What was that?" Nicola backed away from one of the openings.

"What?" Jonathan leaped towards her and shined the pen light down the passage. There was nothing to be seen as far as the light revealed.

"I saw something move, I'm sure of it." She took Kyle's arm as he approached.

"We're bound to get spooked down here," Kyle reasoned. "We should go back. Maybe come back sometime with a video camera and do a Blair Witch film or something." Kyle hoped the suggestion would convince Jonathan to abandon the adventure. The solid walls were far too closed in for his liking, though he reasoned that at least they didn't appear likely to cave in.

"Kyle's right," Nicola concurred. "There could be homeless people living down here or something. We should go."

"Just because you imagined you saw something?" Kyle didn't like Jonathan's disparaging tone, but Nicola pulled him up on it before Kyle could say anything.

"I *did* see something! Don't try that patronising crap on me!"

"What did you see, Nicola?" Kyle wanted her to know he took her word for it, despite his secret doubts.

"Eyes," she responded. "Large, golden eyes."

Kyle couldn't see Nicola's expression clearly, but the pause in her voice told him that she was genuinely afraid. He put an arm around her shoulders.

"Could it have been an animal? Rats get everywhere."

"This was no rat," Nicola insisted. "It was the size of a man and ran on two legs!"

"Oooookay I'm scared now," Jonathan admitted, though it was hard to tell if he was serious. "Let's go back. I've got the train schedule written down so we can wait just inside until it's clear."

The group stayed close together, shuffling back towards the passage opening they had come through while Jonathan moved the light around constantly as if he were looking for monsters in the shadows. They turned right at the opening into what should have been the first passage they had followed through the fissure in the wall, but just a few steps ahead of them it dead ended.

"What the hell?" Jonathan asked no one in particular.

Kyle felt his stomach constrict and he started taking shallow breaths.

"This is the right place," he insisted. "We didn't go far enough to get lost. This has to be right!"

"Jonathan, shine the light over here." Nicola closely examined the wall in front of her. Jonathan aimed the pen light on the patch she was scrutinising. Kyle looked over Jonathan's shoulder, his eyes wide, trying to determine what Nicola had found.

"Look," she explained. "It's a random patchwork of layers like you would get from a cave-in, but the rock is solid. Look here..." She pointed at a pattern of zigzagging colour layers. "It's as if the rock has been melted into place!"

"How?" Jonathan's voice had risen an octave. "That would take equipment that makes a lot of noise. Not to mention more time than we were down that passage."

"Maybe we've been here longer than we thought," Kyle suggested.

Jonathan looked at his watch, then pushed a button that illuminated the face.

"Twenty-five minutes. That's all we've been down here. Damn goblins, man."

"Damn what?" Nicola questioned.

Kyle answered instead.

"Ignore him, he plays too much D&D."

Nicola glanced at Jonathan, then addressed both boys together.

"Okay, let's try to be sensible about this. How do we get out?"

Nobody said anything for a moment, then Jonathan made a suggestion.

"Somebody had to make that wall. If there's someone living down here, human, goblin, morlock, whatever... they have to have another way out.

"What if..." Kyle began, then he rephrased his thoughts. "I know I've seen too many horror movies, but if someone lives down here, they're probably not too keen on visitors. Since they're not walking up and introducing themselves, or offering to guide us out, I think we can assume they're hostile."

"Oh gods," Nicola whined. "What if they're cannibals?"

"Don't go all B-movie on us, Nicola." Jonathan turned the pen light in Nicola's direction.

"You're the one who mentioned morlocks!" The glare in her eyes just caught the fading pen light illumination before Jonathan dropped the beam to the ground.

"We can't afford to argue amongst ourselves," Kyle interjected. "We have to think clearly. Find a way to get out." Despite the cool underground temperature, a drop of sweat from his forehead slid into Kyle's eye, stinging with its saltiness.

"Kyle's right. I'm sorry Nicola." Jonathan sounded genuinely contrite. "We're all a little scared."

He thought for a moment, then continued.

"We can't dig through that rock and wandering around in a labyrinth of caverns would be stupid, so we follow that sound and see if we can spot anyone to follow. Keep quiet ourselves."

"What if the sound turns out to be some machine?" Kyle asked. "That won't do us any good."

"It's music," Nicola stated. "Listen..."

Kyle strained his ears and noted that the cadence had changed, albeit subtly. Somewhere behind the slightly irregular beat of what he agreed sounded like drums, a high-pitched note sounded, followed by others. Something resembling a flute, he decided.

"They'll have the advantage." Kyle didn't like the sound of his own voice saying it, but the evidence was inescapable. "They'll know their way around these tunnels. We don't. They probably know every sound that belongs to this place and... the one Nicola encountered means they know we're here."

"Thank you voice of doom!" Jonathan bellowed. "If we get out of here alive, I'll make it up to you guys."

"It's not all your fault." Nicola placed her hand on Jonathan's shoulder, comfortingly.

"Yes, it is," Kyle fumed, immediately hating himself for saying it. "He's right though, we have few choices now. Let's follow the music and see where it takes us. If it's a party maybe they'll have food."

Nobody said it out loud, but Nicola's comment about cannibals crossed everyone's minds. Mention of food didn't sound so appetising in its wake.

They moved as quietly as possible, following Jonathan's pen light beam down the tunnel where the drumming got louder. Kyle hoped he wasn't the only one who noticed that the beam was getting fainter. What would they do if the batteries ran out? The thought of getting trapped in total darkness underground made it difficult to keep his panic from rising, like the taste of bile in his mouth.

That thought led to a memory of some of the survival information he had picked up from movies. The dank smell of the cavern increased as they walked. If they could find a source of water, surely it would lead to a way out? Or perhaps it only meant that the nearby Thames river seeped moisture into the ground and they were just as likely to fall victim to drowning if the water breached the earthen walls.

Kyle mentally slapped himself for letting his morbid thoughts take over. He needed to keep focused on thinking clearly and finding a solution. Apart from anything else, saving them all would make him a hero in Nicola's eyes.

The dimming penlight sputtered its failing light.

"Oh no..." Nicola whimpered.

"I've got it covered," Jonathan assured her. He took a package of new batteries out of his back pocket and held it up in the remaining light.

"I may be idiotic but I'm not stupid." Jonathan used the pen light to note the positive and negative ends of the new batteries, then turned it off for a moment and changed the batteries by feel. A few seconds later, it came on again with a strong beam.

Kyle let out a breath he had held through the brief period of total darkness. He turned to look over his left shoulder where Nicola had been standing, then felt something in his stomach drop.

"Where's Nicola?"

Both boys looked all around, Jonathan moving the light about frantically.

"Nicola!" he called in a loud whisper. There was no sign of her. They had heard nothing.

Kyle began to babble.

"What'll we do..."

"Don't panic.

"What'll we do!"

Jonathan grabbed Kyle by both shoulders.

"Don't. Panic!"

"We have to find her!"

"And how do you propose we do that?" Jonathan reasoned.

Kyle felt his bottom lip tremble and his eyes moisten.

"We keep following the music." Jonathan kept his voice stern, in control of the situation. "Find out where they gather, and we'll find her there."

Kyle had no better plan. He nodded agreement, trusting Jonathan would see the gesture, now that they had sufficient light. He couldn't trust his voice not to crack. They continued through the tunnel they had been following. The music continued to grow louder as they went. Jonathan kept the light mostly on the ground to minimize announcing their presence around any hidden corners. The caution saved them from walking into a massive pit in the floor, right in the middle of the passage.

They skirted around the chasm, Jonathan shining the light around their feet as they took careful steps. Strangely, Kyle didn't react strongly to the potential drop. He had stood at the edge of an open airplane door too many times on his sky diving jumps to fear heights, though the pool of unbroken darkness within the unknown depths gave him the creeps.

They kept their attention more diligently on the floor in front of them after that, alert for more such traps. Kyle was more concerned about how thoroughly they were becoming lost in the network of caverns and tried to count left and right turns in his head. Jonathan kept following the music. Kyle followed, still unable to think of an alternative plan.

After many twists and turns, they came around a corner to find a glow of light emanating from one of the turns ahead.

"That's where they are," Jonathan assured them both. "It has to be."

"Now what?" Kyle could think of a million reasons to avoid confronting whoever played the music and only one to move ahead; Nicola.

"Here, you hang on to the light." Jonathan pressed the pen light into Kyle's hand. "I'll creep up and see what I can see in there."

"Be careful!" Kyle whispered. The panic began to creep up his spine again.

"I've got years of spying on my older brother and his girlfriends behind me. I can be quiet." Jonathan winked at Kyle and pressed himself up against the far wall, skulking slowly towards the dimly lit opening. Kyle turned off the pen light and backed into the relative safety of the darkness. He kept Jonathan in sight, watching as he moved nearer the dimly lit opening.

By the time Jonathan reached the edge where he could see inside, Kyle could see his friend's face clearly. He watched as Jonathan's expression changed from cautious foreboding to one of sheer horror, his eyes wide and mouth forming the shocked 'O' of a silent scream.

Jonathan broke into a run towards Kyle's general direction.

"Kyle!" he hissed through the darkness.

"Here!" Kyle answered, turning on the pen light.

"Run!" Jonathan grabbed Kyle's arm, fumbling for it in the partial darkness, and pulled him down another tunnel leading away from the source of light. Fearful that they would fall into another pit trap, Kyle pushed Jonathan around the corner of yet another passage, turned off the pen light and covered Jonathan's mouth long enough to get his breath enough to speak in a whisper.

"We're going to fall into a pit or something if we run blindly. What did you see?" Kyle took his hand from Jonathan's mouth and let him get his breath as well.

"There must have been hundreds of them. Monsters! Wall torches like you see in the movies made them easy to see. They looked like Neanderthals with ridges all over their faces, and green! Some had dark tattoos. They were dancing, stomping around to the drums. It looked tribal, really primitive."

"Did you see Nicola?"

"No but... I don't think they plan to hurt her." Jonathan took a deep breath. "I didn't see a lot of females."

"Oh god..."

"There's too many. Even if she'd been in there, I don't see what we can do."

"But we can't just leave her!" Kyle cried, no longer ashamed of the tears streaming down his face in the dark. "We can't just let them..."

Something like a grunt erupted from Jonathan, as if he had been punched in the stomach.

"Jonathan?"

When he didn't answer, Kyle turned on the pen light to see Jonathan's eyes glazed over and blood dripping down the side of his mouth. Kyle took a step back and Jonathan's body dropped to the ground. The handle of a large spear protruded from his stomach.

Kyle began to hyperventilate. His feet tried to run, but he was swept up by muscular arms he only glimpsed as the pen light fell out of his hand. Whatever had him had thrown him over its shoulder as if he weighed nothing and was running down one of the tunnels at a pace that should only have been practical for someone who could see where they were going. He felt his bladder release, though the creature, whatever it was, gave no reaction.

Struggling was useless. Kicking, crying, begging... nothing Kyle could do phased his captor in the least. Then suddenly he was airborne. The echo from his belly-deep scream told him that he had been thrown into one of their pits.

Something inside him curled up into a resigned vesicle of acceptance. There was nothing more the creatures could do to him now. He was going to die. He just hoped it wouldn't hurt too much. What was at the bottom of this endless drop? Flat ground? Spikes? Monsters? He couldn't save Jonathan. He hadn't been able to save

Nicola. They had been his ultimate failure, far beyond his inability to save himself.

He closed his eyes and spread his arms and legs out as if he were in freefall with a parachute on his back during a routine jump and imagined himself out in the bright sunshine of the open sky.

***

"Please, you have to believe me! They didn't hurt me. Jonathan and Kyle might be alright!" Nicola could see nothing but dismissal from the sympathetic smile on the face of the policewoman across the desk. Her story just wasn't getting through. The constable standing next to his colleague walked around to where Nicola sat and leaned his hands on the desk.

"Let's go over it again, shall we?" Nicola had a sudden urge to slap the belittling smirk off his face but getting arrested for assaulting an officer wasn't going to help her friends. She gripped the edge of the wooden desk and gritted her teeth while the authority figure who should be helping her casually read her statement back to her.

"You and your two friends trespassed on the Underground tracks to go explore a fissure in the wall and found... goblins?"

"That's what Jonathan called them." Nicola steeled herself to be patient, though every fiber of her body screamed for urgent action. "They were monsters, hideous to look at. They dragged me away and..."

"You said they took you to a dance?" The two cops exchanged a sceptical look.

"They were dancing, and some were playing drums or what looked like flutes carved from bones. They tried to get me to dance but I refused. Then they forced some nasty tasting fluid into my mouth... it tasted like bad mushrooms... and I pretended to swallow, then to pass out. I assumed it was poison and spit it out a little at a time when they weren't looking."

"Then what happened?" The female cop asked, interested despite her obvious disbelief.

"One of them picked me up as if I weighed nothing and threw me over his shoulder. I was scared shi.." Nicola's gaze flicked from one cop to the other. She decided swearing was a bad idea. "Really scared. I tried to make myself go floppy so they wouldn't catch me out. Then they just left me."

"On a patch of grass on Hampstead Heath," the male cop finished, glancing at his notes. "That's pretty far from Tower Bridge Station."

"If you saw the network of caverns under the city, you'd see..."

"Excuse us a moment." The cop motioned with his head and the woman cop got up to follow. Nicola began wringing her hands together, searching her mind desperately for any piece of information, anything she could say that would lend her tale credence.

A few yards down the hall, the constable turned to his partner.

"I'll call the London Transport police to get them to file a complaint for trespassing. Then we can hold her and see if we can get permission for a full toxicology report. Bad mushrooms indeed..."

"Best check for Ecstasy and all the other hallucinogens too," the woman cop agreed. "Can we get a psychiatric evaluation?"

"I'll talk to the sergeant," the constable volunteered. "We should check out the addresses for her friends too. If they can't be found, we better think about dragging the lake on the heath and any other places a drugged-out teenager might come to mischief." He looked back towards the door to the interview room with a haunted expression in his eyes.

"Poor girl," the woman voiced the unspoken sympathy she saw there. "Her nightmares are just beginning."

The End

Autumn Leaves

Monster Smith

For Joseph Smith

A light breeze cascaded through the neighborhood, sending goose pimples up Leia's forearm like rapid fire. She rubbed at it, trying to dispel the cold as she walked to the next house over. She'd wanted to go as one of the princesses from her favorite films but wound up being a pixie instead. It was her mother's idea, a decision she wasn't very happy with.

"Come on Eliah, hurry up," chirped Leia.

"You don't have to wait for me, you know."

"Mom said we have to stay together," she whined.

"I can't believe I'm stuck babysitting," he muttered under his breath.

"I'm not a baby, Eliah," she said, her feelings hurt.

This was Leia's first time going trick or treating without her parents chaperoning. They had let her go with the promise that Eliah would watch over her the entire time. Unfortunately for him, he was tasked with babysitting his seven-year-old sister, although he'd much rather gone by himself.

Eliah was fifteen years old and looking forward to starting his freshman year in high school soon. He felt he was old enough now that he shouldn't have to keep tabs on his little sister anymore. He had his own life to live, and he would have preferred the company of his friends.

He followed Leia up to the last house on the corner of the street, escorting her to the front door. There were spookily carved jack-o-lanterns lighting up either side of the front door, along with a bloody welcome mat for aesthetics. The owners had switched their normal light bulbs out for black lights, to add to the eerie Halloween theme.

They walked up to the door, managing to avoid the flood of kids receiving their candy. One was dressed as a clown, another as a werewolf, and yet another was wearing a scary looking skull mask to compliment his jeans and plain white tee. Their buckets were overflowing with treats, and Eliah was insanely jealous.

He knew his bucket would be just as full if he didn't have to drag his bratty sister alongside him.

They approached the door and Mr. Park opened it slowly, greeting the kids with a "Happy Halloween" and a smile.

He was an elderly veteran in his late sixties and had been a fixture in the neighborhood for nearly two decades -- a lot longer than Eliah or his sister had been alive. He was stiflingly friendly and was extremely fond of the little ones throughout his neighborhood. He was always polite and willing to help with anything he could. He was slow on his feet, thanks to an injury he suffered back in his military days, and he strode with a limp, never going anywhere without his trusty old cane. Leia smiled back.

"Trick or Treat, Mr. Park."

"Well aren't you just the cutest little thing," he said, all smiles. "What are you supposed to be, a fairy?"

"I'm a pixie," she said enthusiastically.

"I see," he said. "Well, you sure are the cutest little pixie I've ever seen." Leia giggled, and Eliah shook his head to express his displeasure at the small talk. He stuck his nearly barren pillowcase out for his share, thanking Mr. Park once they were finished. It was coming up on eight o'clock - almost time to call it quits. There were a few more streets to cover before they headed home, and Leia was excited to continue the quest.

As they journeyed to the next street over, Eliah happened to run into a few of his classmates, including Cari Worthington, the girl he'd had a crush on since middle school.

Oddly enough, she was dressed as a dancer, wearing knee-high black leather boots, a snug halter top, and the hottest skintight booty shorts he'd ever seen. His eyes bulged out of his head, like one of those old cartoon characters he used to watch on Saturday mornings when he was a kid. He tried to play it cool, offering up a casual, "Hey, Cari."

"Hey," Cari replied. "What are you up to tonight?"

"Oh, nothing really, just getting candy."

"Me, too," she said and held up her bag. "How did you make out?"

"Not too bad," he said. "I'm about half full."

"Yeah, me too. Jane over there, though, is making a killing. This is her fifth neighborhood tonight."

Eliah glanced at the girl's bag and was surprised to see it overflowing. She must have hit every neighborhood in town, he thought.

"That's a killer costume," he said, hoping not to come off as creepy.

"I like yours, too. What are you supposed to be?"

"I'm a mafia hitman. You like the suit?"

"Yeah, it looks good on you," she coyly replied, and shot a smile his way. "We're going down to the old Potter Mill right now. Wanna come with?"

"I'd love too, but..."

"Mom said you have to stay with me," interrupted Leia. "I'll tell on you."

"Shut up. Go away," he snapped, embarrassed and hoping Cari wouldn't make fun of him for being out with his little sister.

"I'll tell on you," snapped Leia.

"It's cool if you can't come," Cari responded, flashing a flask full of booze she'd copped earlier from her old man's liquor cabinet at home. "Guess we'll have to have fun without you." She winked at him, saying "We'll see you later," and disappeared into the shadows around the corner.

It was the first time she'd ever asked him to tag along, and he wasn't able to because he was stuck watching over his snotty little sister. He was sick to his stomach.

"Why do you always have to ruin everything," he barked angrily. "Sometimes I wish you were never born."

"That's mean," said Leia, her eyes watery and red around the edges. "I hate you!"

Walking down the street after hitting a few houses, Eliah noticed a smattering of insects dancing under the streetlights. The air had grown a few degrees warmer and muggy, giving him a weird vibe as they neared the end of the street. There were only two houses left to hit on Clapton Drive; the Thompsons' and the Wicks'.

The streetlight flickered above their heads as they made their way to the last house on the street, the Wicks'. As they drew closer, Leia saw a stuffed scarecrow sitting in a chair by the front door. Having seen those sort of things before, she knew what was about to happen.

"He's going to jump out at us," she whispered to her brother with a smirk.

"Duh," said Eliah, still angry at his sister. "Mr. Wick does the same thing every year."

"You don't have to be mean," she snapped back, her feelings hurt once more. "You're no fun tonight."

"Neither are you," he replied snidely. "Let's just get this over with. It's almost time to go home." Suddenly, as they were arguing, Mr. Wick, dressed in his fake scarecrow costume, jumped out at them.

"Arrrgggggghhhhh," yelled Mr. Wick as he stumbled toward them. Leia was caught off guard, and she just about flew out of her shoes. Eliah had been waiting for Mr. Wick to pounce on them and scare them, and he couldn't help but burst into laughter at the expense of his little sister. She was such a scaredy-cat, easily spooked by her own shadow.

"Good one, Mr. Wick. You scared her good," he said, laughing.

"Shut up, Eliah," she screamed at him.

"Now, now, children," said Mr. Wick through the latex mask. She stuck out her bag.

"Trick or treat," she said, her heart still pounding from the scare. Mr. Wick grabbed the bowl of candy he'd laid out for the trick or treaters and let them each grab a handful. He wished them a goodnight and sat back in his chair, sitting still, playing possum for his next victim. As they finished and began toward the last street of the night, Leia tripped and banged her knee.

"Are you alright?" asked Eliah.

"My knee, it hurts," she said with watery eyes, inspecting it.

"You're so annoying. Get up."

"You're the worst brother ever," she yelled. "I hate you!" They were rounding the block, approaching the last street of the night before calling it quits, when they bumped into Henry Little.

Henry Little was the highly disliked neighborhood bully, who was always getting himself in trouble. He was known for getting into fights and causing destruction, occasionally spending some time in juvenile detention centers.

Recently, over the past few weeks, Henry had taken a strong disliking toward

Eliah. Anytime he saw Eliah around, he made a point to pick on him, for whatever reason he could make up. Eliah had guessed the reason to be that Henry was simply jealous of him.

Tonight, Eliah was completely caught off guard when they rounded the corner and ran into Henry, next to the oleander hedge.

Bugs attacked Henry's neck, and he smacked at them like a mental patient who just escaped a hospital. One of the bugs splattered on his neck and palm, and Henry rubbed the guts on his jeans. He spat at Eliah, hitting his shoe.

"Well, look who we have here," he said, with an evil grin spanning from cheek to cheek.

Eliah didn't know what to do; his main concern was getting out of there as fast as he could. He didn't want his sister around a hoodlum like Henry. She didn't need to be exposed to someone so vile.

"What do you want, Henry?" asked Eliah impatiently.

"Looks like I hit the jackpot tonight," said Henry, laughing manically.

"What jackpot?" asked Leia, catching a nudge from her brother. Eliah glanced down at her and shook his head slightly from side to side, subtly informing her not to say anything.

"Looks like I'm going to be elbows deep in candy tonight," Henry chuckled.

"What do you want, Henry?" asked Eliah once more, waiting for a reply.

"I want your candy, dumbass."

"You can't have our candy," blurted Leia, catching another nudge from her brother.

"I can take whatever I want," he said, laughing as if he'd just said the craftiest thing ever.

"That's stealing," she chirped.

"And what are you going to do about it?" he snarled, glaring at Eliah.

Suddenly there was a grumbling noise coming from their right, amongst the oleander hedge. Out of the blue, Eliah recalled a memory from when he was younger. He was around seven or eight at the time. His Uncle Jimmy told him a story about a monster that lived in the oleander hedges.

His uncle told him of a nasty, quarter-century-old tale about a monster that lived in the oleander hedges around town. He warned Eliah to keep an eye out and never get too close, "or the oleander monster will get ya," he would say. Uncle Jimmy told him that the oleander monster fed on the souls of children and young adults. He said it would eat the bodies of its victims and absorb their souls for energy.

All those thoughts raced through his mind in a matter of seconds, and he took a step backwards, remembering what his uncle had told him. He never really believed in the tales his uncle told, often chalking it up to his warped sense of humor.

The air flexed with anticipation, and bugs circled in droves under the soft yellow glow of the streetlight. Henry paid no attention to the sounds coming from the oleander hedge, instead aiming his aggression at Eliah and his sister. The temperature had risen at an alarming rate over the last minute, as they stood there, sweating.

Henry noticed beads of moisture sliding down Eliah's forehead, thinking highly of himself. "Either hand it over, or I'm going to beat you to a pulp," he demanded.

"Henry, come on man," said Eliah. "Don't take our candy."

"Hand it over or I'm going to smash you up," he said with fire in his eyes. Eliah handed his bag over.

"Here, take mine, but let her keep what she's got. She has nothing to do with this."

"Hers, too," said Henry, puffing out his chest. "Hand it over."

"No. You can't take hers," said Eliah.

"Your choice," said Henry, and he swung at Eliah. His fist connected with Eliah's cheek, and immediately Eliah clutched at the side of his face. His cheek swelled instantly as his face turned bright red.

"What did you do that for?" cried Leia, concerned for her brother's safety.

"Hand it over," demanded Henry. Leia lowered her head, disgusted at the bully, and stuck her bag out for Henry to take. There was nothing she or her brother could do about the situation. It was beyond them. Henry reached for Leia's bag, when all of a sudden, the bushes started moving.

Eliah let go of his face and watched as something breached the hedge, covered in leaves. It was thick and slimy, with dying yellowish green leaves plastered to it like some otherworldly sculpture. Henry had his back to the hedge and couldn't see it stretching for him. Leia saw it coming and stood there slack jawed, staring at the thing in awe.

Without warning, the thing grabbed a handful of Henry's shirt, yanking him into the oleander hedge. Henry screamed at the top of his lungs, but there was no one in sight to help. He kicked and punched at the thing, trying to get free.

"What the fuck?" he yelled. "Help me! Help me!" The thing drug him into the oleander hedge, disappearing amongst the leaves. Eliah couldn't help himself and just had to see what it was that grabbed Henry. He parted the hedge and peered in, trying to get a clean look at the thing.

It was made up of gooey grey mush, with leaves stuck to it like skin. Deep crimson, vine-like veins twisted all over, just under a layer of leaves. Eliah watched as the thing opened its slimy, saliva drenched mouth and bit down on the top of Henry's head.

There was a sickening crack as Henry's skull was split open by the monster's powerful bite. It chomped and chewed on the skin and bone, smacking its mouth, enjoying the delicious meal. Eliah was mesmerized and couldn't seem to pull himself away.

Henry's left eye opened, looking right at Eliah, as he gurgled and choked on his own blood. Skin and tissue fell from the monster's mouth as it continued to eat. Henry's leg twitched, kicking out at the air, and Eliah knew he was dead.

Leia managed to get her head under Eliah's arm, wanting to see what was happening. She saw the monster and instantly started screaming. It startled Eliah, breaking him out of the trance he was in.

"Get back, Leia," he yelled.

"Oh my god," she cried. "Is he dead?"

"Don't look! Don't look, Leia! Stay back," he said in a state of confusion.

Henry raised his arm, reaching for help, and the monster snapped down like a bear trap, taking a bite out of his exposed brain. It looked like spaghetti smothered in sauce, and Eliah couldn't stand to watch any longer. He let go of the hedge and bent over, putting his hands on his knees, trying to gather himself.

All of a sudden, he heard Leia screaming and turned around just in time to see her feet disappearing into the hedge. The thing had grabbed her and drug her off into the oleanders. As scared as he was, he mustered up all the guts he could and parted the hedge, searching for his sister.

The monster was holding her in the air, its dripping, gooey claws clenched tightly around her waist. It looked at Eliah, almost smiling, like it knew a dirty little secret that he didn't. It tilted its head, as if to get a better angle, and opened its mucky mouth, ready for the next course.

"Get away from her," he yelled in a panicked frenzy. "Leave her alone!"

"Eliah," she said, drowsy, half conscious, her eyelids drooping. His mind was spinning this way and that, and he had no clue what to do. But he knew he had to get his sister. He summoned all the grit he could and forced himself into the oleander hedge.

It felt like a sauna inside the hedge, and Eliah quickly became disoriented due to the dense humidity. Henry's body was lying on the ground next to the monster, half eaten, discarded like a chicken bone.

Half of his head was missing, and his right arm was nowhere in sight. Blood and chunks of brain matter were sprinkled all about like cookie crumbs.

He made eye contact with the monster, catching its gaze as it paused what it was doing. It had shiny yellow eyes with black, vertical pupils, like a cat. Its eyes were hypnotizing and frightening, like the eyes of some unknown ancient race. Its mushy wet skin was crawling with worms, cockroaches, and various other bottom feeders.

Eliah wiped the sweat from his brow as the insects swarmed like vultures. The monster stretched its mouth wide, taking a bite out of Leia's neck, splashing the surrounding leaves with blood. He could see the life draining from his sister, and knew he had to do something quick.

The monster munched another mouthful of Leia's neck and instantly her head drooped, as she slipped into a state of unconsciousness. It had a voracious appetite and continued to gorge itself on the body of his sister, as he watched in terror.

"Leave her alone!"

The monster raised its head, staring right at him, as pieces of flesh and bone tumbled out of its mouth. It continued to sloppily chew with its eyes firmly fixed on him, never once wavering. Blood poured from Leia's head wound, washing her face with a mixture of grey mush and sticky red liquid.

Suddenly, Eliah heard voices coming from the other side of the hedge, and his heart raced at the prospect of help. It sounded like trick or treaters on their way to the next street over, probably the last of the night. He was already late getting home, and he knew that soon enough his parents would start looking for him and his sister.

"Help!" he cried out, but there was no response. "Someone help me!" He turned back just as the monster took another chunk out of Leia's neck, dripping blood like gravy.

The thing was hideous, a forgotten obscenity, an abomination of mankind. It roared at him with an unquenchable, ravenous hunger that couldn't be satisfied -- no matter how much it ate.

There was nothing left he could do for his sister; she was already dead. He turned to leave, fearing for his own life, not wanting to be the creature's next feast. As he tried to exit the hedge, ruffling and squishing sounds drifted over him like a lullaby. He glanced over his shoulder one last time and saw the atrocious monster, two feet back. He grabbed at the hedge frantically. Just as his hands touched the leaves, he was yanked backwards into an infinite darkness.

Red and blues lit up the street as men in uniforms meticulously raked over the crime scene. Cones were placed at either end of the street, blocking any traffic, and yellow caution tape surrounded the oleander hedge.

"Hey Pranke, come take a look at this," said one of the officers.

"Damn Jameson, I've never seen anything like that before," replied Officer Pranke, parting the hedge.

"I've got a child over here; a female," said Officer Jameson, inspecting the body.

"I've got two more over here; males, teenagers," said Officer Pranke, wiping the sweat from his face. "One's missing a head. Anyone see a head around here?"

"Look at this," said Officer Jameson, touching a slimy grey spot on the shirt of the headless body. Officer Pranke started toward the street, when all of a sudden there was a ruffling behind him. Out of the corner of his eye, he saw something coming at him, followed by a sloshing sound.

The End

King Brokkos' Revenge

Daren Callow

If he had been that way inclined, Douglas Brown might well have been enjoying the early evening as he trudged in his grimy army fatigues across the edge of yet another muddy field. The evening chorus was expending the last energy before retiring with hearty abandon as the ochre sun cast its final light of the day across the rolling hills. But Doug was not all that interested as he concentrated on the metronomic sweep of his metal detector and awaited a beep that might indicate his evening had not been entirely wasted. It had been a bleak and frustrating few days, since he'd found the fragment of gold torc last month, which had sent his selfish greed into overdrive. It was a piece of an incredible Celtic jewellery, much out of place in these Sussex fields, but a tantalising possible glimpse of the mythical King Brokkos – rumoured in Celtic legend to have fled a family feud and founded a debauched society in the far south of the county. Legend had it that harmony of sorts had endured for a few years, until eventually greedy locals, who lusted only for his wealth and power, had betrayed the king to his bloodthirsty kin. An epic final battle ensued, which the king was said to have won before dying of his wounds and being buried in secret, presumably with his great wealth alongside him, in the foreign lands he called home. Quite a story, if any of it was true.

Doug, of course, knew full well that he should have reported the find, turned it over to the antiquities committee, but nothing could have been further from his mind, and never had been for all the coins and fragments of relics he'd found before. After all, he was born and raised in the county and considered anything buried there to be his by right. With the torc, not knowing how to get any value from it legally, in the end he'd crudely and unthinkingly melted it down. Passing if off as so much scrap metal to a dodgy jeweller who was complicit enough to ask no questions. Easy money he thought, like so many other antiquities he'd disposed of, but since then he'd stomped illegally around many an adjoining pasture, dodging farm hands and hikers alike, with no results. It was probably getting time to turn it in for the day, head back to his car and get some rest, but like a gambling addict who keeps pressing the spin button, he kept swinging his detector over another clump of ground. There was always that chance that this next swing would chime with the tell-tale beep that was the sign of the plunder he was seeking.

He'd been so lost in his concentration that he suddenly realised the evening had all but slipped away and the sun was below the horizon. There was no moon tonight and the light was disappearing like a thief into the night. A slight worry shuddered through him as he realised he might struggle to find his way back to his car. Still, he always had his phone: find any road and he'd figure it out. He stumbled as it was becoming very hard see where his feet were falling. Cursing under his breath he reluctantly reached into his camo jacket pocket for his head torch. Should have put it on sooner. With his metal detector balanced on his leg, he fumbled to sort out the straps. Whilst doing this a loud crash and snort from the hedgerow alongside his field alarmed him and he dropped the torch.

"Fuck it,' he muttered, out loud this time, his pulse racing, wondering what had caused the commotion. Probably just startled woodpigeons, or a lost sheep; they made the weirdest of noises. In the near pitch black, he knelt and fumbled for his head torch, but frustratingly he couldn't find it within arm's reach on the cloying soil. "Fucking stupid sheep,' he cursed a little louder, hoping to scare it off if it was lingering nearby. He could do without more frights. He was about to take off his headphones to look further, when the detector fell away from his leg, letting out a loud and insistent "peeeweeep" as it did. By luck, rather than judgment, it seemed he'd literally stumbled into something. His adrenaline surged, and he tried to grab the falling instrument but instead lost his balance tumbling over against the ground with an awkward thump. A searing pain shot up his arm and he yelled out in agony, rolling over onto his left side, grabbing his right arm. "Fuck!" he muttered through gritted teeth, he'd really hurt himself badly. The pain was absolutely searing, he'd probably dislocated or broken something important. He dragged in great mouthfuls of damp air, trying to calm himself. The pain was so intense that it was hard to think, but he had to calm himself down and work out what he was going to do. Breathing hard, he lay there on his back for a minute or so, gazing up to where a myriad of tiny stars were flickering in the night sky. Shame there was no moon tonight, that at least would have made things a little easier.

The pain in his arm seemed to have calmed down into an intensely numbing dull ache, so he began to put together a plan – which was nothing more than gather up his stuff and find the nearest road. To this end he pulled his headphones off his head, now caked with dirt, and tugged on the coiled lead to try to get his detector, but it was clear straight away that the lead had come out and was no longer attached. He'd run out of curses at this point, so he figured it was time to stop feeling sorry for himself anyway. Dropping the headphones, he reached into his trouser pocket for his mobile phone. At least with that he could set a GPS point to come back, use the torch to find his kit, and then make his way back to the car. After that he could decide whether he needed A&E or not; he just hoped the phone had some charge. Painfully, he held it in his right hand and tapped at it with his left. No signal, but half a battery charge at least, thank fuck for that. He fumbled for the torch icon; it took him two goes to get it on and wave it round to orientate himself a bit. Before he could do anything else, and without warning, there was a crashing, snarling sound from the undergrowth and a large, wild-eyed, striped-faced creature lunged at him, clearly trying to attack the light. He screamed and kicked out as hard as he could, thinking that perhaps he'd made contact with it. The animal let out an inhuman screech but thankfully backed off. Panicked beyond rational thought, he tried to stand up as the torch light flicked dizzily across the field, but with only one arm working he couldn't find his balance and fell again. Feebly he held out his left arm to break his fall, but rather than stop him it went through some brush and he continued to fall with a sickening lurch, headfirst, into a deep hole. Earth and branches crashed around him, as he fell at least six feet and landed hard on his shoulder onto a stone surface. He covered his eyes as seemingly endless amounts of dirt and rocks cascaded over him, covering his legs and most of his torso.

When the earth had finally finished falling, he lay, half on his side, gasping in deep breaths. He was prone on a series of cold stone slabs; the air was rich with damp smells of soil and musty animal odours. The pain in his right arm returned with a vengeance, causing him to grimace and grind his teeth. He let out a long guttural moan, as much to mitigate the pain as anything. He realised after this that despite the shock of the attack and the fall, he'd somehow managed to hang on to his mobile phone in his left hand. At this point he was grateful for small mercies. He brought it up to his face and tried to use his thumb to turn on the torch, but the screen was caked with mud and it didn't work no matter how hard he tried. Still, the phone screen was giving off a faint glow and that was something at least.

Using what little luminosity that produced, he moved the phone around to explore out his circumstances. He was lying in what seemed to be a small flagstone-lined tunnel, perhaps two feet wide or a little more. His feet and lower legs were covered with soil and the tunnel looked blocked with fallen earth, but the other way, as far as he could strain to see, the passageway carried on, perhaps into a larger room. His mind was in overdrive now as, from his little knowledge of ancient burials, this appeared to be the entrance to a burial cairn. This possibility caused his heart to thump a little harder, as he realised that perhaps, despite everything, he'd stumbled on the last resting place of the fabled King Brokkos. At this point it seemed far too good to be true, and probably was unless he could find a way to get out. Looking at his phone screen he sighed as he realised he still had no signal, so no chance of calling anyone. Not that he knew who to call anyway. Looking in vain one more time he could see that there was definitely no way out the way he'd fallen in, so the only course was to go onwards and see what lay in store for him. He thought, somewhat optimistically, that perhaps he detected a slight breeze from somewhere, so maybe there was an easy way out. Looking forward in the eerie phone light glow he saw the flag stones were mostly clear with only the odd animal dropping and what looked, rather alarmingly, like fragments of bone. He also realised pretty quickly that with only one good arm he couldn't crawl and hold the phone, so he carefully buttoned it into a jacket pocket. This done, he began to shuffle forward, one or two painful inches at a time towards where the tunnel opened out. Trying to ignore the foul smells and the odd things, both hard and soft, he felt on the tunnel floor.

Using this method of crawling until the pain got too much and then checking carefully with his phone, he finally made it into the larger area. With an extreme effort he pulled himself up into a sitting position and got out his phone again to illuminate his surroundings. This time he let out a little gasp as the light from the little phone sparkled off bright metal items in every direction. The room itself was a total mess, some large creature having obviously made a nest down here. Scattered here and there amongst the twigs and nesting material were pieces of what he assumed were metal, pottery, fragments of bone, and so much more - it was almost too much to take in. Dug into the wall were niches which tantalisingly promised to contain more valuables, or perhaps what was left of the bodies buried here.

The chamber was only about five feet high, but perhaps twice as long so he might be able to stand if he was careful. At the far end there were at least two further tunnels, roughly similar in dimension to the one he'd just hauled himself through. If he had any luck left, one of them might be a way out. Despite his predicament though, all he could think of was what money he might be able to make from the burial goods in the tomb. Flashing the light around again he felt that he could make out reflections of both gold and silver and possibly gemstones amongst the detritus. All his bloody Christmases had come at once, assuming he could find a way out that was. Still, one thing at a time. Putting his phone safely away again, he cautiously began to stand up using his good arm and the wall for support. He then took one tentative step into the room and was relieved to find solid stone amongst the litter. So far so good, and throwing all thoughts of patience carelessly aside, he swung his other foot forward to step further in and kicked something hard and extremely sharp with it. He had no time to feel pain as he lost his balance again, trying to grab the wall found no hand hold and he crashed back down onto the floor, his fingers scraping the wall uselessly.

As he recovered his breath, he knew he really didn't feel too good. There was pain in his left ankle now, a different kind from his shoulder, and instinctively he reached down to feel it with his hand. It didn't feel right at all - there was clearly a deep wound and his hand now seemed to be covered in something wet and sticky. Fumbling for his phone, whilst trying to stay calm, he turned on the phone screen to see that his hand, and the phone, were now covered in a red liquid. A metallic taste came into his mouth as he realised it was his own blood. Flashing the light from the phone towards his ankle he could see a red stain across his trousers and trainers, which seemed to be growing steadily. At that moment he felt very faint and fought back the urge to throw up. As this passed, more tentative investigation found the cause of the wound; what appeared to be an intact and extremely sharp sword that was lying across the floor wedged into a pile of broken sticks. It was also covered in his blood, but despite this he pulled it out of the rubbish and stared at it in disbelief. He'd never seen anything like it in his life, the absolute bloody find of the century, it seemed to him to be in perfect condition. Turning it over in his hand he took in the fine metalwork and the, still pretty much intact, badger head on the hilt. He knew from the legend that the badger was King Brokkos' own personal symbol. Without doubt he'd won the fucking lottery, if only he could get out alive to make the most of it.

Another wave of faintness swept over him and prompted him to attend to his ankle. It seemed to still be oozing out blood and the cut was deep and dirty. It really looked quite shocking and his stomach churned with queasy sickness again. He had to think but his swimming head made this very difficult. Thoughts slowly hammered their way through his headache. He must stem the flow somehow, anyhow. Fumbling clumsily around, and despite slippery wet hands, he used the little light he had and the newly appropriated sword to cut some strips off his t-shirt and tie them as tightly as he could around the seeping wound. Every part of him felt full of pain now and his head swam again as the throbbing threatened to rupture a vein in his temples. With a shudder he thought he might lose consciousness, but somehow managed to fight it off. It was becoming clear now that he had to prioritise getting out over his overwhelming instinct to gather booty. First, he needed light, so with a piece of his t-shirt and his own blood he desperately wiped the face of phone and tried the torch icon again. This time it worked, flooding the small chamber with white light and he found himself looking straight into one of the niches, which sure enough held a gleaming white skeleton. Straps of leather and metal around its limbs showed it to be a person of status. Indeed, if the size of the torc around its neck meant that he hadn't found King Brokkos himself, then he was a Chinaman.

Before he was able to look any further there was an alarmingly loud noise of something scurrying towards him down one of the tunnels. Panic and alarm flooded his veins and, switching the phone to his near useless right arm, he grabbed the sword handle in his left. There was a growl and a crash as the animal entered the chamber, its face a mask of snarling teeth and wild eyes. Its forehead was striped with black and white, and red, fresh from a kill. Its nostrils flared and snorted as it inhaled the scent of the helpless man's blood. Before he could even scream, it leapt for him, sinking its teeth into the flesh of his flailing right arm. He did let out a bloodcurdling yell now and swung the sword desperately, his phone falling away, sending garish, flickering shadows up the stone walls. The beast came again, strong and determined, and as it bit him, he hacked down with the blade. This time there was an unearthly howl as the wounded animal first tightened its grip and then, after what seemed an age, let go and ran for one of the tunnels. Douglas fell hard, his head swimming and stars flying before his eyes. The phone had somehow landed with the light facing upwards and, as he lay dying on the floor of the cairn, he found himself staring into the leering hollow eye sockets of a skull. Its striped helmet, worth a king's ransom no doubt, still more-or-less in place. "Fuck you," spat Douglas as his vision started to fade, "fuck you all." But despite his resistance, the aching in his heart told him he was gone.

His very last thoughts as his precious crimson blood drained into the earthen floor made him emit a bitter chuckle. One day, who knows, the burial chamber might be found and the excavators, be they fellow low gravediggers or respected archaeologists, would scratch their heads with equal wonder as to how the modern man had come to be dead, sword in hand, half eaten by wild animals amongst the fallen of another age. They would never know the truth, that in the end, King Brokkos, thousands of years after he'd been committed to the earth, had had his final revenge on at least one of the descendants of the men who had betrayed him.

The End

Feed the Earth ... It's Hungry

R.C. Rumple

The howl was unlike any he had ever heard around the settlement or the surrounding forest. The shrill tone had pierced the night as the moon cast its eerie silver glow over the trees and underbrush. It was a reminder to Jason that guard duty had just become more dangerous. As the population of humans dwindled and that of the creatures of the forest multiplied, the odds of surviving grew less. Only too wary of the fact, he hoped one day to be a part of changing the future back into man's favor.

The wars were ancient history ... one that no longer mattered. To awaken each morning was the primary goal of each human living in a world tainted with radiation. The bombs and man's inability to properly man nuclear power stations had led to the contamination of the orb, ironically called Earth. Those who remained cared not about what led to the destruction ... as it served no purpose to their immediate future. Instead, the priority of how to face wildlife which had grown fearless of man mattered most.

Jason stared into the darkness, his senses on full alert, in hopes of seeing any hint of the owner of the howls lurking about. His rifle, readied for firing and held in his sweaty hands, followed his scan of the area. Its normal position, slung across his shoulder, made it easier to carry, but the warning of the howls had made the change necessary. Behind him, thirty-two people slept deep in the dampness of the cavern. He presented the only defense between them and possible death.

The group had done well in reinforcing their stronghold. The entrance to their hole in the ground had been fortified with rock and packed tight with earth. Only a small entry way remained. This was to be blocked at night by a blazing fire to keep animals at bay. With only a small flame lingering, Jason realized more wood was needed. Yet, to do so would mean laying down the weapon. With the howls so close at hand, it was an act Jason feared chancing.

When they had first gathered together, they had resided in the buildings that had survived the carnage. Rats and mice had attacked in mass quantity, consuming the corpses of the dead. At first, they had done so at night. Yet, as time progressed, they grew bold and made it a daylight activity as well. Their taste for human flesh had grown. None could survive an onslaught of hundreds swarming. With no other options, humans had left the cities seeking safer lands. Only the rodents had remained behind. Soon, snakes and birds of prey, seeking a food source, joined them in the concrete jungle and feasted on their flesh.

Everything goes in cycles.

Small groups of survivors fled first to the farmlands, and then to the hills surrounding them. They had first made homes of the eighteen-wheeler trailers. It was thought the tin floors, walls and ceilings would protect them. Instead, the containers had become inescapable prisons as the larger predators simply waited until the doors opened. It was then the bears, panthers, and wolves had charged in and ravaged the flesh of the helpless. The few surviving had done so only by fleeing as the screams of those being ripped apart faded behind them.

Most believed total annihilation would be imminent. To force themselves to work in the fields to grow crops became more of a struggle each day. Still, there were those who believed they would make things work. They pushed Christian beliefs of man beginning as two ... Adam and Eve ... being the sole occupants of a similar world filled with dangers. If they had succeeded, even after having fallen from God's grace, then today's group could as well. It was their motivation. Yet, one debated with anger by those who believed God had turned against mankind and was reeking vengeance for their evil acts.

Movement, off to the left of the cave's entrance, caught Jason's attention. He focused, hoping to catch a glimpse of what had caused the lower branches of the thickets to sway back and forth. The form of a wolf would be easy to make out ... especially one large enough to have earlier echoed such a powerful howl. If it was not a lobo, the wolf would have other pack members circling about.

Glancing up at the rock overhang ... he exhaled a sigh of relief at its impenetrable presence. It would make a topside attack impossible. Not having seen or heard anything for several minutes, Jason decided to chance taking his eyes off the ominous darkness of the forest and get the fire going full strength, again. Holding onto the rifle with one hand, he tossed a small log upon the fire with the other. Sparks shot up from the impact and smoke filled the air. His eyes burning, Jason hurried to add two more before turning his blurred gaze back to the outside. If he was lucky, the beast out there would be backing off. None would be brave enough to face the fury of the flames. He kicked himself for ever allowing the fire to die. In his will to be wary, he had almost provided an opening for the creatures of the woods.

Jason's mind flowed to the various creatures they had seen since the Earth had been poisoned. Besides those common before the apocalypse, there had been mutations. Most believed them to be results of the radiation that remained ... radiation that would forever be their unwanted companion. Most mutations had been minor, but there was one that made the animals twice as dangerous. The animals had doubled in size.

Jason had never seen but had heard the tales of group members working in the fields and being carried off by gigantic wolves. Without warning, the animal would appear at full run and snatch one up. Before help could come, the victim had been carried off at breakneck speed to the cover of the forest.

He had no reason to doubt the stories being told. Only two weeks before, Jason had seen a child playing close to the cave entrance. From the sky, a monstrous eagle swooped down, grasped the young boy in its hooked claws, and carried him off. Jason remembered how ironic it had been to hear the cries of the youngster fade as he was stolen away by the bird that had once signified human freedom.

And, only a few evenings ago, there had even been the huge python ... over forty feet in length. It had slithered into the area and made its way toward the cave. Luckily, the roaring sentry fire had stalled it from entering until the bullets did their job and ended its efforts. Although not common occurrences, these events had brought about a sense of reality. Not all was going to be as they had known it to be. The unexpected was now to be expected.

Another howl interrupted the quiet of the night. Jason shuddered as the chill of its sound brought goosebumps. This one had been close and off to the right of the cave. The animal was either pacing back and forth ... or had an accomplice. Jason's fear heightened his need to secure the cave entrance even more. Watching the darkness, he reached out for another log and fed the fire to raise the flames even higher. The burn of the heat scorching the hair on his arm held no concern. It would grow back--but only if he were still alive to see it.

A sudden scratching atop the rock overhang sent down a dusting of loose earth, landing near the front of the fire. Yes, there had been great wisdom in choosing this cave for the group to reside. Not only was the sentry safe from topside attack, but so was the fire. Still, Jason had to shake his head as an epiphany struck. This was another example of a mutation. Most animals were clearly instinctive. Yet, the knowledge that loose dirt would douse a fire's flames took intelligence. Clearly, the foes they now faced not only were born with their natural instincts, but with increased intelligence and logic as well.

New questions originated from this fact. How much more dangerous could the creatures become if this was true? Already, it had been observed that the wolves had improved upon their pack skills and attack techniques. So had the rodents. What if the same thing was happening to the reptiles? During the day, when the entrance fire was extinguished, a mass of venomous serpents could enter the cave and envenomate every living soul within. No solitary guard could throw up any sort of viable defense. And, if the birds of the sky were changing as well, tomorrow might bring a scene reminiscent of an old horror movie he had seen as a child.

How could mankind survive if the creatures of the world became as intelligent? Without the natural weaponry Mother Nature had given animals, intelligence had been mankind's saving grace. Yet, by the same train of thought, intelligence had also brought about mankind's demise. Could it do the same to the animals?

Jason pondered the questions. Already, the growing hunger of bird and serpent populations had gone after the rodents in the cities and eliminated most. What if the birds attacked the humans and serpents in mass as well, or even the wolves? Could eagles, vultures, owls, and other predatory animals of flight become the new rulers of the planet? And if so, for how long before they ate themselves out of existence?

The politicians of the past would scoff at such a thought. Yet, that was the same reason they only occupied the past. Their insatiable hunger for money and power, and their beliefs and practices, had brought about their attitudes of callousness. Pursuing this greed, they had ignored the warnings ... their egos blinding them to the fact mankind wasn't invulnerable. They lived only to feed their pockets and egos.

At first, a society ... starving for the basics needed to live ... had protested their leaders feasting. When their attempts failed to wake up the politicians, various groups proceeded to random acts of violence. Of course, government leaders had ignored the reasoning behind the acts and sent in the armies of police and military to control the masses.

Being masters of deception and misdirection, politicians continued to ignore common sense. They fed lies to the media in efforts to divide the powers working against them. Even in a state of disruption, these developing "herds" were easier for them to control. Each could be directed to battle the other, instead of those in charge. The concept of working for the good of mankind became passé. Instead, each herd was fed ideas and "facts" to intensify their energies to benefiting their own group alone.

Political acts of deception then came into play on an even greater scale. Mimicking great illusionists, they mastered the skills of diverting attention. By getting the herds to focus on one direction, the politicians could do as they pleased from another. The results were frustrations growing and the people becoming much more desperate.

Unbelievably, the politicians continued their false façades. Their deceptions, evident at last to even the most devoted and blind, no longer satisfied the hunger of the people. The first "dirty bombs" exploded next to the Capital building in Washington D.C. during the final president's State of the Union Address. As the bombs exploded, the brief images of the politicians' faces in disbelief were broadcast ... and laughed at. More radioactive devices were exploded the next day. New York, Chicago, Atlanta, Los Angeles ... all were blasted into the melee. The military, assuming control with the politicians now dead, reacted as expected. Claiming foreign intervention, nuclear missiles, supposedly once disarmed, were sent to the skies. Targets in other nations fell. Those able to retaliate did so with passion.

Jason shook his head, remembering those final days ... days of normalcy as they had once been called. The ensuing panic with the loss of mass communication--television, radio, and Internet, all destroyed--had set the direction of the future. A route of destruction followed as mass panic and violence became the norm. Those, who had protested the ownership of weapons, found themselves regretting their past stances. Helpless to defend themselves, all they could do was watch their homes being robbed and hope they weren't killed in the process.

But that had been long ago. Now, the first signs of the horizon were appearing. Within an hour, dawn would take place and his watch would be over. Jason no longer had to strain to make out shapes ... the early light of day making them easier to distinguish. Still, there was danger in believing daylight would bring safety. Too many of the naive had died under the light of the sun's rays. The only difference between night and day was the ability to see what creature might be eating you.

Jason took a deep breath and exhaled. His feeling of being alone departed as there were sounds of activity deep within the cave. Some of the older members would be stirring and preparing to begin another day ... wondering if it would be their last. They would partake of the remaining fruit harvested yesterday, freshen up in water from the hot spring inside, and then gather outside to shed the cave's dampness from their bones. Later, the children would wake and do the same.

He would be relieved and would sleep most of the day. His was not a responsibility of hunting or gathering, but one of protecting those in the cave as they slept. The night was Jason's to guard, while another did the same during the day, and a third the early evening. There were twenty-nine others to do the rest of the work.

The rays of the sun broke over the horizon and sent darkness home to sleep. The forest still held mysteries, but one could now see if they drew near and prepare. Slinging the rifle on his shoulder, Jason relaxed and leaned against the cool stone wall of the cave. To his relief, he would pass on the information of the howls and hope others exiting the cave would be on the lookout for whatever had sung them to the night. He didn't want to wake later and hear the news of another losing their life. They were too few already.

The smoldering fire now added its smoke to the morning haze. It spoiled the freshness of the day's new air but would soon die out. All would awaken ... some would have hope this day would provide a glint of hope for the future. They would fight the mental battle of daily survival with optimism. It was all they had ... all else had been lost.

Jason only wanted for his relief to show up so he could get some sleep. The night had been stressful and had worn him down. He rubbed his arms, still aching from holding the rifle in the ready position most of the night. His relief was late ... later than ever before. It was odd ... almost as if he'd forgotten. Yet, stoic in his need to protect, he maintained his post, repeatedly telling himself, "Have patience. He'll be here soon."

As the sun rose over the trees, the birds made their appearance, ate their worms, and left to enjoy their day. Still, there were few noises from inside the cave. It was as if the whole group had decided to sleep in and not told him about it. As his weariness grew, so did Jason's frustration. If I'm counted upon to be at my post on time, I expect the same of the others. But, no one else is here either. Usually, most would be out in the sun and preparing for their day's work. There should be many sounds of activity inside by now. What could be going on? Something's not right.

He had waited long enough. Jason decided he would break the rule of deserting his post. It was an unforgivable act, but an exception had to be made. There was no other option. There were too many things out of sorts ... routines being broken. It wasn't his imagination at play ...

something was amiss. If the folks inside were in danger of some sort, he could be of help. And, if all did turn out to be fine, he could always present the argument he'd maintained his defensive position between the outside and the cave's inhabitants.

Taking the rifle from his shoulder, he turned and crept inside. Although the morning was bright and sunny, the walk into the cave's interior eliminated the outside light after the first turn. Lying ahead was a foreboding blackness ... one that could hide the evilest of foes ... be it man or beast. Knowing the wall torches should have been lit by now added to his eerie dread. Running his hand along the wall as he proceeded, Jason pulled the first torch he came to from its holder and lit it. The flames igniting sent his adjusting vision reeling. Giving his eyes a moment to focus, he gathered his courage and repositioned his rifle. Should he be attacked, he wanted to at least get off a shot.

The cave's main living area was getting near. He continued to light the wall torches as he went. The illumination they provided was somewhat comforting. He realized it being only a sense of false security at best, but it kept him going. Finally, he lit the last wall torch before the main room. As the flames filled the cave with light, he wished he hadn't.

In front of Jason was the reason for the lateness of his relief ... a scene of inescapable horror. Partially eaten and disembodied torsos and body parts littered the cave floor ... now sticky with their blood. Heads of those he had shared bread with stared up at him with unblinking eyes ... yards from their bodies. Even the children had been savagely murdered ... ripped apart ... their heads mounted atop stalagmites like trophies. Innocent and happy kids, with whom he'd joked, would laugh no more.

Jason could stand no more. Every member of the group had been torn to pieces as they had slept. His head spun from the ruthlessness exhibited. Rushing to seek exit, he slipped and fell to the blood saturated earth below his feet, now a red mud. A friend's open torso greeted Jason's face. Blinded by his friend's bloody wounds, a rush of panic flooded his body and Jason scrambled to locate the rifle he had dropped on the way down. His fingers frantically sought the gun's metal barrel or wooden stock but found only puddles of blood. The hole in the Earth which had been their home was now the earth his friends would call their grave.

He had to get out before he could call it his.

His mind raced. I was on guard all night. No person or thing got by me. How could this have happened? We've searched and searched, but never found another way in? Could the creatures of the night have succeeded where we failed?

A howl, like the ones he had heard only hours before, echoed deep from the rear of the cave. Adrenaline surged and logic retreated. Leaping to his feet, Jason stepped toward the entrance, catching his foot in the sling of his rifle. Stumbling, he again crashed to the earth of the cave floor and spun back to find the rifle. There, against his fingers, was the cold touch of its metal barrel. Grabbing it up, he aimed to the darkness. Maybe, just maybe, I can get a shot off and kill the beast before it gets me!

Waiting for any sign of movement, he was distracted by a scratching from above. Claws were digging into the outside earth ... claws wanting to reach him and end his life as they'd ended the lives of all the others. Aiming at the ceiling, he fired. The bullet ricocheted from the stone and narrowly missed him as it entered the soft earth below. Then, another howl ... this time from the back of the cave ... much closer this time. He pointed his rife into the dark and shot again ... the bullet careening along the rock walls and traveling into the never-ending blackness.

His pulse raced and forehead pounded. Somewhere in the darkness was the beast ... or, was it above him? He had to find it. Yet, ammunition was running low. He had to be careful not to waste it.

The panting of an animal behind his head and the drip of saliva upon the nape of Jason's neck told him the ammunition mattered not. The creature was too close. He would be dead before he could pull the trigger. Jason smiled. Damn wolves ... just like the politicians, get me thinking they're coming from one direction and hit me from another.

Razor sharp teeth sunk deep into his skull and shook it with incredible strength. Vertebrae snapped and muscles ripped. As his head went flying, Jason's body slumped to the earthen floor of the cave. A solitary howl of victory signified the plight of man's existence had ended.

For a final time, the Earth tasted human blood. It found justice to taste the blood of those who work to destroy you ... those who cannot live in harmony. As the remainder of Earth's creatures eliminate each other, more blood will feed the Earth. As populations dwindle, the Earth's hunger will decrease. One day, there will be no more blood to feed upon. The hunger and vengeance will be satisfied.

The Earth will save itself.

The End

There Is Only A Hole Here Now

Zachary Ashford

A solitary maggot wriggled and stretched its grotesque little body up and out of the girl's tear duct. Its pearlescent hue glinted in the sun and Jau watched it locomote across the bridge of her nose. Fat and peristaltic in its clumsy side-wind of a gait, it plopped to the ground and disappeared in the wet mud and detritus. The thick and cloying smell misted, musty and redolent like stale piss. Revolting bile flooded into Jau's gullet with the taste of half-digested chocolate milk and school-canteen meat pie. Hot and acidic in his throat, it lapped somewhere behind his barely formed Adam's apple, threatening to erupt in a viscous fountain of puke. She had strips of flesh missing. Sinewy strands of muscle dangled like spaghetti. Claw marks like those you'd see on the cover of an old horror movie lacerated her face and arms. There was chewed flesh. Broken bones.

Ryan pressed the back of his hand against his nose. "That's Haley," he said, "That's Haley from school."

"No way dude, how could it be her?" Sandy leaned over the corpse.

Jau waved a fly away from his face.

"Have you seen her this term? I haven't."

Using a twig, Sandy lifted a shock of mud-stained hair away from her face. "Man, we need to call the cops. No, call my mum. She'll know what to do."

"Don't be stupid, Sandy. She's got maggots crawling out of her face. Call my Dad. Tell him to come get us, then call the cops."

"What if they think we did it?"

"Murdered a girl and left her near our treehouse?"

"I'm going to be sick, man. I'm not even allowed to watch television after six-pm. I shouldn't be seeing this."

"Then go away, Ryan. Go away and be sick or stand here and hold it in like everyone else." At the thought of vomit, Jau's stomach went queasy. If Ryan threw up, he'd have trouble holding onto his own guts. They chucked, he chundered. It was a thing.

"Let's go. Please," Ryan said.

***

Shortly after rollcall, Jau looked up from his worksheet when he heard Mrs Martello speak. "Sandy McAllister," she said in her no-nonsense voice. "Return to your seat at once, thank you." She observed Sandy's actions with a monstrously patient eye, but Sandy turned the computer on without looking at her. "I'll give you sixty seconds to make the right choice before I issue you with a detention."

"What's going on with him?" Jau asked Ryan. Sandy wrestled a thick green booger from his nose, wiped it on the screen and eyeballed the teacher.

"I don't give a shit," he said. Later, when he came out of the deputy principal's office and found Jau and Ryan in their spot outside the library, he yanked a sandwich out of his bag and bit into it. "Mum's marrying that douche-bag, Adam." He crammed the remaining half bite into his gob. "She's gonna move us to Perth."

"She can't."

"I think Jau's right; your mum can't take you away without your dad's permission."

"No shit. That's why she's going to court. Adam has money."

***

That night at dinner, Dad polished off his beer and immediately opened the next one. Using the handle of his knife, he popped the cap and let it clatter to the floor. When it finally stopped spinning and fell silent, he leaned forward, his shirt pressing into his baked beans.

"You don't even have a boyfriend; when the hell do you get pregnant?" Ellin looked down and nibbled her corn. Mum made herself scarce. Dad swigged.

"You're not having it." Ellin stood, sliding her chair back with her legs.

"D'you hear me?" Dad said. "You're getting it fucking aborted."

"I hate you! I hate you, I hate you, I hate you." Her bedroom door slammed, and Dad turned his gaze to Jau. "What the fuck are you looking at?"

***

The next day at school, Jau found it almost impossible to phase out the teacher-librarians as they contemplated the ins and outs of Haley's murder. He scrunched up a ball of paper and tossed it into the bin then leaned across to whisper in Ryan's ear.

"They think her Dad did it too."

"Are you even listening?" Ryan asked. "We can't hang out after school because the chess competition's on." Jau separated the nib of his biro from the plastic casing and held it up to look through it.

"Why don't you blow that chess shit off?"

"Because I can hang out with you guys the day after tomorrow."

"Why not tomorrow?" Sandy asked.

"Violin." Ryan's shit-eating grin stretched from ear to ear. "There'll be people from the State Youth Orchestra there. I want into that."

***

Eventually, Saturday cycled its way around and Jau and Ryan rode to Sandy's house. His mum sent them into his backyard caravan with a plate full of sandwiches.

"We should build another treehouse," Jau said. Sandy scanned across television channels.

"No way. We can't even use the one we have."

"There are other ways to build treehouses," Ryan said. "What about a foxhole or shack?"

"What's a foxhole?" Sandy plucked one of the sandwiches from the plate.

"A hole in the ground. You put a roof on it. Build benches and shit into it."

"Sounds awesome," Sandy said.

"We have to destroy the treehouse first." Jau grinned at them.

"I'm sure we can cannibalise a lot of it for use in the foxhole."

"And of course," Jau said, "We'll also make sure no one else benefits from our hard work. That's our treehouse." He picked a poppy seed from his teeth. "No one else gets to have it."

***

When Dad hung up the phone, he turned to Jau. "Who else does your sister hang out with?"

"I don't know." Six beers down, he snatched his car keys off the kitchen bench.

"Bruce, no," Mum said.

"If you ever bothered to get your licence I wouldn't have to." She stepped in front of the big man.

"Things are hard enough without you getting a second DUI." He shoved her out of the way and threw the keys at Jau.

"You can drive. About time you learned."

"I'm thirteen."

"What if whoever got that little slut from school gets her?"

"Okay, okay, just let me check the skate-park."

She was sitting on a bench in front of a backdrop of juvenile graffiti with Veronica and a few guys from school. They had cheap cans of pre-mixed vodka and cigarettes in their hands. Her legs were draped over a guy in chinos and a Dickies shirt.

"Ellin, Dad said you've got to come home."

"No way. He doesn't give a shit about me."

"He's already shoved Mum. Thinks whoever got Haley will get you too. Just go to your room or something." One of the guys stood up.

"He can't do that."

"Sit down, Joe." She kissed him on the cheek. "I'll see you at school tomorrow."

***

"I had a phone call from the State Youth Orchestra. They want me to audition." Ryan hovered outside the crime-scene tape.

"That's awesome, dude. When is it?"

"A couple of weeks. It's in the city."

"You'll smash it. You're a gun." He stepped closer to the treehouse. "Feel like someone's been here to you?" Ryan blocked his nose with his hand. "It smells like animal piss."

"You think the cops are coming back?"

"Fuck the cops," Sandy said as he retrieved a little hatchet from his backpack. Whereas Ryan's instrument was the violin, Sandy's was his rage. He threw the sharpened tool and the blade thudded into one of the load-bearing branches used as a beam. It wobbled there, shuddering.

Jau poured petrol siphoned from his Dad's car into an empty ice-cream container and pulled a plastic bag full of polystyrene from his backpack. He snapped and crumbled chunks of the polystyrene, dropping it into the container, watching it react and melt into sticky goo. He sat an old trowel and a stolen lighter beside the mixture. Ryan shook his head.

"You can't set fire to it. We need the logs."

"We'll chop more trees."

"That's a waste."

"Pussy. Sandy is totally up for chopping down trees right now." *Look at his eyes,* Jau thought. *He wants to watch the whole thing burn every bit as much as I do.*

On the upper levels of the treehouse, Sandy hacked into a branch with his hatchet. He smashed the zip-ties used as hinges for the rusty gate posing as a door and stepped back.

"Watch out!" He kicked it with pulsating glee, and it crashed into the shrubbery. "Is that napalm?"

"Do Catholic priests fuck little boys?" Jau asked, scooping up a wad of it with the trowel. Sandy jumped down, clumsily fell over, brushed grit from his knees, and laughed as Jau spun the lighter-wheel and flames engulfed the gunky mixture. Sparks sputtered as the projectile fizzed through the air. It landed with a splat and fire crawled up the dry bark.

They took turns throwing the burning substance at the treehouse and held a bonfire to celebrate their youthful frustration with their shitty lives. In the middle of preparing a gob of napalm to hurl at the already burning treehouse, Ryan stopped and pointed.

"What the fuck is that?" There, visible through the shifting flames, staring with malevolent eyes, a hulking thing loomed. Jau shielded his eyes and squinted at the shape beyond the smoke, flames, and burning timber. Every primitive fibre of his body wanted to run. Just run and run and run. His body screamed it at him, but he couldn't turn; couldn't pivot. The thing's head jerked sideways. Then it dropped low, disappearing from sight.

"What in God's name are you little bastards doing in here?" The cop strode towards them with a cocksure grin on his face. "This is a crime scene," he said. "You boys are in shit now."

Ryan stammered an answer while Jau tried to relocate the monster. Only a branch swayed back and forth where it had stood.

"It's gone."

"And so should you be. Grab your bikes and get up to the bloody road before this whole bloody forest catches fire."

***

When the news started, Jau's old man put his belt away. He didn't even bother with the usual lecture. He grabbed another beer and watched the reporter share the remains of the boys' handiwork – the blackened husk of a treehouse – on the television. He swigged; wiped his mouth.

"You little wanker." All Jau could think of were Haley's wounds, the maggot crawling out from the corner of her eye and the thing at the treehouse. The next day, when he and Sandy got to Ryan's place, Jau knocked three times and did a full lap of the front and back doors before giving up. They found him at school, comfortable in the library.

"What's the go, dude?" Jau asked. Ryan shifted.

"My parents are driving me from now on."

"Why?"

"I can't hang out with you anymore."

"That's bullshit," Sandy said.

"I told them that." *He didn't. He never stands up to his parents.*

91

"So, we can only see you at school?"

"Yeah, but Mum asked my teachers not to let me sit next to you in class."

Jau groaned. "This sucks a fat one."

"Why would they do that?" asked Sandy. Ryan rolled his eyes.

"The bitching fire we had last night, Sandy. The cops took us home. I'm grounded forever. Hell, I'll be lucky if I'm even allowed to audition for the orchestra at this point."

"What about the treehouse?"

"There is no treehouse, Sandy. We burned it down."

"What about that thing?" Jau asked. He had to keep it fresh in his memory, so he didn't forget it completely. The general shape and ominous size of it wouldn't leave his mind, and neither would its eyes. The fine details, though? They were gone.

"The flames played a trick on us," Ryan said. "We imagined it."

"We didn't. Not all of us." The visceral image of Haley's mutilated body and the smell of stale piss in their newly blackened treehouse hadn't escaped Jau's memory yet.

***

Back at home in his bedroom, Jau tried to avoid attention while his father tore into Ellin again.

"You're nothing but a whore and you won't be having it under this roof!" Jau looked up from his sketch when she ran past his room.

"I'll have to leave," she said when he knocked on her door. Wet tissues marred by mascara and tears were piled on the bed next to her.

"He'll come around," he said. "Mum won't let him kick you out – especially with a baby."

"Mum said she might get Auntie Kylie to take me. She's been lonely ever since Uncle Phil died."

"Where is Mum? I haven't seen her all day." Ellin checked the hallway, and then quietly pressed the door closed.

"In bed. She doesn't want you to see what he's done to her. She thinks it'll teach you it's okay." Jau made a fist and gently pressed it against his own face before opening his palm in a questioning gesture. Ellin nodded and hugged her brother close.

***

The next few days were quiet. Still grounded, Jau was putting the finishing touches on another drawing – his best yet – of the monster, when he heard screams in his sister's bedroom. He dropped the red pencil and ran to her. She scrambled against the wall, a wash of blood between her legs, clutching her stomach. "Get mum!"

He burst open the door to the master bedroom, something they were never supposed to do. "Mum! Ellin needs you!" He snatched the phone up from beside her bed and called the ambulance. When he went back into his sister's room, his Mum sent him out.

"Just grab a bag and pack her toiletries," she said. "I'll pack her clothes."

***

The day after, Sandy went to the city for the court-case, but Ryan should have been there, fresh from his audition. He'd been told he might still be able to go if he could stay out of trouble.

Jau got through the day without going completely mental, but after school, he stopped by Ryan's house to ask how the audition went. Ryan's older brother Jonathon answered the door.

"Come in, Jau. Come in." He led Jau to a seat at an expensive dining table. "Ryan is in hospital. Dad crashed the car on the way back from the audition last night." He paused when he saw the tears running down Jau's cheeks. "Ryan's okay, but Dad's on life-support. I'm going to meet the rest of the family at the hospital soon."

***

On the way home, Jau cycled past the outskirts of the forest. Even from the road, he could see the burnt patch where the treehouse used to stand. The police tape strung across the walking trail flapped lazily in the breeze. Buffeted by the wind, it had stretched and warped. It hung loose. Dirty. He slowed down, and tried to look beyond it, imagining the thing he saw through the flames – fur matted and shaggy, shape hulking and ominous – tearing the tape down, inviting more victims into its territory.

From the pathway leading to the treehouse, a flock of birds shot skywards. In their wake, the monster, ponderous and massive stepped forward. It cocked its head to the side as if listening and then levelled its baleful eyes on Jau. Bigger, far bigger, than the largest man could ever be, it dwarfed the boy, even from this distance. *Pedal. Just fucking pedal. Get out of here.* The thing jerked its head towards the intersection a few hundred metres back the way Jau had come, then turned and loped back into the trees. The revving of a car engine cut across the breezy afternoon air. He let it pass then pedalled for home.

When they arrived at the hospital, Sandy and Jau raced ahead of their mothers. Inside the room, Ryan sat motionless on a plastic chair. The curtain drawn, an IV drip bled slowly into his father's arm. Ryan's mother and two older sisters stood around the bed as Jau approached. Ryan looked up, eyes red-rimmed and tear-stained. A wave of heavy sobs rolled over him like the tide. His shoulders heaved and dropped, and the salt-wash trickled down his cheeks.

Sandy and Jau stared at each other; hovered wordlessly. Jau couldn't bring himself to approach Ryan's dad. Instead, he rested a hand on his friend's shoulder. Ryan held him and cried into his shoulder before turning back to his sisters. Jau and Sandy lingered for a few more moments, awkward and unnecessary intruders on what should have been a private occasion, before his Mum wiped a tear and damp foundation from her bruised cheek. Ryan finally spoke.

"Will you pray for him?" he asked. What could he say? He sure as hell couldn't announce that every time he closed his eyes, he saw that thing staring back at him. "I will."

With the air full of burning humidity, Jau constantly wiped sweat from his eyes. When they stopped to drink from their frozen water-bottles, Sandy finally opened up about the court-case.

"The judge said Mum can only take me if Dad agrees to it." Unsure how to respond given everything else that had happened over the last few days, Jau opted for a fist-bump.

"I'm really glad, man. I'd hate to lose you."

***

Two days later Ryan returned to school. He found Jau at the library while he waited for Sandy to finish his detention. The big goofball might have had some good news, but his mum hadn't stopped pressuring him. On seeing Ryan, Jau ran to him and hugged him like an excited puppy. Another kid leaned out of the tuckshop line and cupped his hands to his mouth.

"Why don't you pussies save your love-fest for your little cubby houses?"

"For your information," Ryan said, "that's where we trace the lineage of all the students at this school. Apparently, your parents are actually brother and sister."

"The fuck?"

"He said the same thing your fringe has been telling us for years, Mark. You're an inbred fuckwit." Mark grabbed Ryan, the smaller of the two boys, and threw him to the ground just as Sandy strolled around the corner with a plastic bag half-full of rubbish in his hands. He dropped the bag and pushed Mark away from Ryan.

"You want to fight?" Mark raised his fists. A fringed pugilist. Sandy ploughed a big fat fist straight into Mark's pointy nose. He didn't stop swinging until the teachers pried him off.

***

Ryan's dad died that night. Jau dreamed of the shambling creature. He wondered if Ryan did too.

***

Sandy returned from suspension and after a few days of grieving, Ryan wanted to ride to school with his friends.

"I want to dig a foxhole," he said as they rode. "Take back our treehouse. Now the Haley thing's over, you know." *Those wounds. That thing.*

"You really think they did it?"

"Parents murder their kids all the time," Ryan said. The police tape still dangled there, and the thick smell of musty piss had settled on the area like a fog. Around the blackened frame of the treehouse, a claustrophobic air hung; silent without the usual cacophony of birds. Jau hesitated.

"We shouldn't be here."

"You still think there's a monster here?" Ryan asked, stepping off his bike and unslinging his bag from his shoulders.

"You saw it first, Ryan. Don't be a dick."

"I saw a shadow. A fucking hallucination from the smoke in the air." He walked into the very centre of the charred copse of trees where the old fortress once stood. "Where are you?" he screamed. The afternoon breeze washed through the canopy.

"Come on, Ryan. I don't want to be here either." Sandy monitored the foliage around them with concern etched onto his face and his arms folded.

"Then fuck off, Sandy. Go home and leave us alone."

"He's right, Ryan. We shouldn't be here. Can't you feel it?" Ryan drove a shovel into the ground, right in the centre of the thicket.

"We're digging a foxhole here." The scratching of the shovel seemed louder than it should in the closeness of the afternoon. Something rustled in the trees ahead of them. Silence dropped, cloak-like, on the gathering and the thick, musty piss-stink grew stronger. The thing exploded out of the foliage, growling and slavering, charging into Sandy, driving him against the trunk of a tree with the rampaging force of a careening vehicle. A splintered and stubby branch punched through the meaty flesh of his lower back and burst out of his belly. Jau saw his friend's intestines stretch and bulge across the exposed limb.

The thing, mind-boggling in its aspect, slammed a bear-like paw over Sandy's wailing mouth. Its stygian black claws raked across Sandy's throat. Blood spewed. The repetitive thud of Ryan's shovel grew louder, more rapid. He dug. For some reason he dug while a monster tore his friend limb from limb. The last few years of Sandy's life, his parents had split him in two and now this thing was literally dismembering him. The creature stretched the boy's shoulder to breaking point. The sinews snapped, and the ligaments around his exposed socket wriggled in shock like insects under an upturned rock. The smell of piss mingled with the stronger smell of blood and Jau felt a warm wetness run down his leg. Amidst the snarling, the screaming, and the infernal scratching of the shovel striking soil, the monster turned and levelled its gaze on him.

A gunshot boomed. The monster roared at the sky; an unholy baying, and a second report echoed off the trees. It thundered again, and the creature turned tail and fled. Sandy's mutilated corpse sagged awkwardly, still propped up by the branch impaling it. His blood coated the charred trees. His arm lay on the ground by his feet.

The same policeman who'd busted them on the day of the fire wrapped an arm around Jau and held him tight for a moment before checking on Ryan, who stood knee-deep in the hole he'd dug. Jau puked. Ryan kept striking at the soil with the shovel.

"How did you know?" Jau asked between sobs. Visibly shaken, the cop said something into his walkie-talkie before answering. "A passing car saw you heading in with your tools." He looked at Sandy's corpse. "I wish they'd called sooner."

Ryan's shovel struck the ground again. Subtly, the scent of freshly turned earth added to the metallic rancour of Sandy's blood.

"You boys need to come with me. You need shock blankets and I can't leave you here in..."

"In the treehouse?" Ryan's shovel finally fell silent. "There is no treehouse." He sat on the lip of the hole he'd dug. Jau tried not to look at Sandy, putting an arm around Ryan and facing the other way instead. It didn't hide the smell of blood or musty piss or broken soil, but he couldn't stare at Sandy's lifeless eyes any longer. Ryan shrugged Jau off.

"There is only a hole here now," he said. Jau shook him, but the boy who played the violin so well didn't falter. "There is only a hole here now," he said. "There is only a hole here now. Say it, Jau. Say it. You know it's true."

Jau rested his forehead against his friend's. *He's right. The treehouse is gone. The earth is broken. There is only a hole here now.*

"There...is only...a hole here now." It came out like a whisper, but Ryan pressed against him, crying.

"There is," he said, louder this time, "Only a hole..."

"Scream it, Jau. Scream it." He grabbed Ryan's shirt, pulled him close, and bellowed so loudly he could feel his vocal cords tearing. "There is...only... a hole...here...now."

The End

Mamaw's Beast

David F. Gray

I stood in front of the old Independence house, trying to layer the memories of a long dead childhood over the reality of the present. There had been changes, of course. I knew that there would be, after nearly fifty years.

In my memory I saw a large, two-story wood-frame house with white walls, bright green shutters and a wide front porch. The house I was looking at was much smaller. Time does that, I guess. The walls were still white, although the paint was blistered and faded, and most of the shutters were missing. The gravel driveway had been paved with cement, and the huge oak tree that had once shaded the wide front yard was long gone.

The Beast was still there.

Five decades ago, it had risen out of the cellar, although that was never its true home. It was my grandmother who recognized it for what it was. It had stolen something precious from her, but she was a tough old bird. She knew things...secret things...and she was not without power. For almost two years, they fought. She had managed to hurt it but, in the end, it killed her. After that, we moved out.

I stared at the old house, letting my memories flow. The Independence of 1964 had been a typical small country town. About twenty miles south of Cincinnati, it sat in the Kentucky high country, surrounded by tree-covered rolling hills. There had been a drug store, complete with a marble soda fountain, a barber shop, a hardware store and two small grocery stores.

A Walgreens had replaced old man Henderson's drug store. The barber shop was closed and boarded over, and the hardware store had been put out of business by the Home Depot franchise that occupied several acres on the other side of town. Still, the old town had the same sleepy quality I remembered as a child.

The earthy aromas of the country washed over me as I stood next to my BMW. It was late in May and the honeysuckles were in full bloom. Their sweet scent complimented the smell of manure from the cow pasture a quarter mile away. I jammed my hands into my pockets and walked past the house into the back yard. Like the house, it was smaller than I remembered, but essentially the same, although the garden that once supplied my family with fresh corn, tomatoes, string beans, carrots and potatoes was now an empty, weed infested plot of land next to the freestanding garage. Visions of countless birthday parties, pot-luck picnics and winter sleigh rides piled into my mind.

The memories grew so thick that I felt as if I was smothering under their weight. I returned to the front yard and stepped up onto the porch. The wood creaked under my weight. As promised, the key was hanging on a nail next to the front door. *Country folk,* I thought, shaking my head. Even in this day and age, it seemed that the citizens of Independence left their doors and windows unlocked. With a last glance over my shoulder, I opened the door and went inside. My vision blurred. I staggered, as if the floor suddenly buckled. The last thing I remember was falling.

* * *

When I came to, I was lying on the hard, wooden floor, staring up at the plaster ceiling. I had fallen hard, banging the back of my head. I groaned and gingerly prodded the large lump that had formed there. Wincing at the pain, I sat up and tried to make sense of the world. *Why did I come here? Why?* The question rattled around in my mind, but I knew the answer. I had been *compelled* to come here, just as I had been compelled to buy the vacant house. Behind me, the door was still open. It had been mid-afternoon when I had arrived, but now it was dusk outside. The small living room was shrouded in shadows. I squinted at my watch and saw that over three hours had passed.

I desperately *needed* to leave. Scrambling to my feet, I stumbled outside and stood on the porch. The crickets were in the middle of their nightly serenade and it seemed as if a million fireflies were hovering over the front yard, flashing on and off like twitchy Christmas lights. I stared at them for a long time, willing myself to get into the car. I don't know how long I stood there...certainly long enough for the evening light to fade completely... but eventually I went back inside.

There was no power, but there was ample moonlight streaming through the wide living and dining room windows. The floor creaked under my feet as I went into the kitchen. It was pretty much as I remembered it. I turned around, and in a single heartbeat, forty years rewound and a memory, long repressed, lit up inside of my mind.

I see myself sitting on the kitchen floor, playing with my wooden blocks. Dad was at work, and Mom and Mamaw were down in the cellar, canning vegetables. Mom calls for me to bring her a glass of water and a clean towel. I grab both and start down the stairs. The next thing I remember is Mamaw carrying me back into the kitchen. I was screaming, my face bright red with the effort. Mom is right behind, yelling at Mamaw to put me down. Mamaw sits me on one of the kitchen chairs and kneels in front of me. Her blue eyes are twin pinpoints of fire. Looking into them, I feel as if I am burning.

I snapped back into the present, shaken by the vivid memory. That was the moment, I knew. That was when Mamaw became aware of the Beast.

Now, the door to the cellar was shut and latched. Just to the right of it was the staircase that led up to three bedrooms and a single bathroom. I stared at the door, unwilling to move. I was sure that the Beast would hear me. It was down there. After all this time, it was still there, waiting.

It took a long time. Finally, keeping my eyes off the door, I eased across the kitchen and went upstairs. At the top, I took a quick look around and then went into my old bedroom. Everything was the same, and yet it was all different. The small closet, the big windows, the high ceiling; it took several seconds, but I finally managed to pull the pieces together and remember the place I had spent a large portion of my childhood. I opened the windows and let in the night air.

Downstairs, the cellar door rattled. I froze, knowing that I was trapped. There were only two ways out of the house, and they both ran straight past that door. It rattled again and then opened with a long, high-pitched squeak. I stumbled over to the far corner of the room and slid to the floor, wrapping my arms around my knees. The Beast was coming for me.

The stairs began to creak, as if bearing a heavy weight. Then the noise stopped abruptly at what I thought might have been halfway up to where I crouched. A moment later, three rapid squeaks sounded out. The Beast retreated. I heard it moving about in the kitchen until, after an eternity, the cellar door opened and closed.

I stayed in my room the rest of the night. All was quiet, but I fancied that I could hear the beast moving about the cellar. Again, I tried to force myself out of the house. I desperately wanted to go back to New York and reclaim my old life, but the insidious power that had compelled me to leave my adopted city and return to the place of my birth now compelled me to remain in that house. I cowered in the corner, and sometime around four in the morning fatigue won out over terror and I dozed off.

The movers arrived the next day. For a while, I was able to forget about the previous night as I arranged my furniture. The power company called to let me know that there had been a mix up and that they would not be out for another two days. I blew up over this. The girl, Charlene was her name, tried to stay calm, but I'm good with words, especially when I'm mad. I had her in tears by the time I was through. I ended the call and threw my cell phone across the room. Then I stormed out the front door. I decided that I would find a motel near I-75 and spend the night. In the morning, I would leave Independence forever.

I stepped off the porch and gasped. My eyes blurred and I could not breathe. My heart thudded against my chest and, for a moment, I was sure that I was having a heart attack. I groped my way back into the house and slumped down onto the living room floor. The Beast had made it clear. I was not going anywhere.

That night I lay in my bed, waiting. Around three, I heard the cellar door shake. Then the latch fell away and it creaked open. Footsteps sounded through the kitchen and into the living room. For over an hour the Beast wandered through the first floor, knowing full well that it was tormenting me. Finally, it started upstairs. I counted the squeaks, and when it had almost reached the top, it stopped. It waited there for a long time. Then, as if deciding to prolong my agony, it returned to the cellar.

I got up at daybreak and for some insane reason, opened the cellar door. I peered into the darkness, wondering just what I was doing. The damp, cold, stale air made me shiver. I must have blacked out for a second. I blinked and found myself halfway down the stairs. With a whimper, I scrambled back into the light. The rest of the day I spent

moving about the house. I could not remain in any single place, and I could not leave. The Beast's hold on me was now so strong that I could not even step out onto the porch.

The third night came, and I went to my bed. The hours dragged on and eventually I fell into a fitful sleep. Suddenly a loud thud rattled the house. I jerked awake, heart pounding. The stairs creaked and groaned, and I realized that the thud had been the cellar door slamming open. The gloves were off. The Beast had finished teasing me. It was coming.

I counted the squeaks, and at twelve I knew that the Beast had reached the top. Harsh gray moonlight was coming through the windows, bathing everything in a surreal glow. A shadow fell across my bedroom door. I stared at it, unable to scream. The shadow moved. It entered the bedroom and glided over to where I lay. Then it sat down on the bed. I felt the mattress move and heard the bed frame creak. I stared at the apparition, if apparition it was. Its hair was pulled back into a tight bun, and its skin was wrinkled with the weight of years. Its face turned toward me, and even in the darkness I recognized its features.

"Mamaw," I whispered. The apparition nodded. I think she smiled. "Mamaw, is it you?" My grandmother nodded again. Then she reached out and touched my arm. Her skin was warm and dry, and the touch comforted, rather than frightened, me.

My fear vanished. The Beast was gone! Somehow, my Mamaw's spirit had exorcised it from the house. I was free! I reached out for her, but she stood and walked over to the door, beckoning for me to follow her. There was no way that I could refuse her. I was on my feet in an instant, following her dark form downstairs.

The cellar door was still open, and she went through it. I hesitated, but her call was too strong. Groping in the darkness, I felt my way down the stairs. There was just a hint of light coming from the window wells over the stationary tubs. It was a small space, only about fifteen feet long and twenty feet wide. The handmade wooden shelves that had once held dozens of mason jars filled with preserved fruits and vegetables were in front of me. Behind me were the stationary tubs where mom and Mamaw had done the laundry. The sup pump stood alone to my right, silent in the dry season, and the furnace squatted in the opposite corner. I was barefoot and shirtless, wearing only sweatpants. The dirt floor was cold and rough against my bare feet.

Another memory tickled the back of my thoughts. It felt important, and I tried to draw it out, but it flittered away. I could now sense a great barrier deep in my mind, blocking something that I desperately needed. I tried to breech it again, but it held firm.

Mamaw stood in front of me. She took my hand and led me behind the shelves. Understand, there was no 'behind'. The shelves were flush against the cellar wall, but when she drew me over, I saw a narrow crawlspace, barely a foot wide. It was both real and not real, and the effect was quite disorienting. At her silent command, I got down on all fours and began to crawl. The grainy dirt bit into my hands and feet.

I squeezed into the narrow there-not-there space. A few feet in, I discovered a tunnel. The opening was small, perhaps only a yard or so square...just big enough for me to crawl into. The tunnel burrowed into the back wall, disappearing into the darkness. Again, memory tugged at me, but I ignored it. I hunkered down and went in.

I don't know how long I crawled. The tunnel twisted and turned so many times that I was soon confused beyond hope. The darkness was complete; a palpable, irresistible weight pressing down on me, threatening to crush me out of existence. I kept going deeper and deeper into the earth, heedless of whether or not I would be able to get back to the cellar. Part of me knew that this tunnel could not exist, just as a part of me knew that it did. As I continued forward, I was assailed by one undeniable fact. *I had come this way before.*

I could feel the memories now, dammed up behind the barrier in my mind. Soon, I knew that barrier would shatter and I would remember. Until then, all I could do was keep crawling.

I came upon the end of the tunnel unexpectedly. I felt, rather than saw, the sides fall away. I reached above me and felt nothing but cool air. Cautiously I stood and found that I was in a dry open space. There was a rustle behind me, and I knew that Mamaw had arrived. I could not picture her crawling through the tunnel, but it did not matter. I felt safe with her there. After all, she had vanquished the Beast.

Light blazed up, blinding me. I cried out, covering my eyes. There was no sound, but the light seemed to come at me from all directions. It ripped at me, its very essence assaulting me from every side. It *hurt*. I tried to squint through my fingers. My eyes adjusted a little, and I could see that I was in some kind of dome or rotunda, about fifty feet in diameter and maybe twenty feet high. The walls were red stone, roughhewn and covered with symbols that I almost recognized.

"Mamaw," I cried out again, desperately trying to find her in the blazing light. Suddenly my skin began to smolder, and I screamed from the pain.

"Now, demon, you will pay." Her voice was harsh and inhuman. It reverberated off the walls of the rotunda and I screamed again. I whirled around, uncovering my eyes, and found the source of light. Mamaw stood behind me, blazing with a power that I could not bear to look at...*and a power that I recognized.* Her eyes were aflame with fire. Her mouth opened impossibly wide, and her voice blasted at me from every direction. The smell of my burning flesh rose to choke me.

"Mamaw!"

"Silence demon," she shouted, and I felt my tongue cleave to the roof of my mouth. "You will not call me that. You will not dare defile that name." Invisible hands grabbed me, and I was flung against the far wall of the rotunda. The stone itself burned me. I tried to scream again, but my mouth would not open. Mamaw glided forward.

"Now, at last," she said in that awful booming voice, "I have you. By the power of your enemy and my ally, I bind you forever." Invisible fetters clamped themselves on my arms and legs, pinning me to the wall. Unbreakable yet invisible chains wrapped themselves around my torso, squeezing me so hard that I was sure that I was going to be cut in half.

"Mamaw! *Please.*"

"I said be silent! There is the only one who had the right to call me by that name. You took him. He was the most precious thing in my life, and you *devoured* him." The barrier in my mind cracked and splintered. In an instant, memories long repressed returned. I remembered who I was. I remembered *what* I was.

I was immortal. I was forever.

I was the Beast.

I was from beyond...beyond the world, beyond the universe, beyond reality itself. I was as far above the pathetic creatures that roamed this ball of mud as they were above the worms that crawled within it. I was nearly all powerful, but...

The last piece of my memory snapped into place. I had a great enemy. We had fought beyond time and space. I was defeated. I was chased across creation itself until I was caught. I was crushed, *compacted*, and imprisoned in this very rotunda. My nearly infinite power was stripped away.

I remembered millennia of scraping and scratching at my prison walls, seeking a way out. My enemy had beaten me but had been weakened by our fight. My prison was not perfect. Finally, I found a crack, the tiniest of flaws. Through it, I found a small town, a small house, and a small boy. I called to him, led him to this prison, and then, slowly consumed his soul. I used his body to escape my bonds.

But something went wrong. The boy's memories, his thoughts, his *heart*, were strong. The longer I lived in his body, the more I became him. My...*his*... parents never suspected, but Mamaw knew. She bided her time until, just after my twelfth birthday, she made her move. She almost succeeded, but I remembered just enough of my true self to destroy her. Even so, her final blow had been her most devastating. In a single deft move, she had managed to block my true memories behind the barrier I had only just now sensed. For all intents and purposes, I had become the boy.

Mamaw never gave up, not even in death. Her spirit hovered in the Independence house for decades, patiently waiting, growing stronger with each passing year. She kept the house from being destroyed just as she kept anyone from living in it. Finally, she drew me back. Now, she had me.

I strained against my bonds. Mamaw stared at me, and the power within her seared me. I recognized it for what it was. Somehow, she had forged an alliance with my enemy. I cried out, begging her for mercy.

"Did you have mercy on my baby?" Her voice cut and flayed me. "No, you will never take another soul, demon. If there truly is a final judgment, and if there is any justice, it will be my hand that delivers you into oblivion. Until then, may you rot in this prison."

I screamed again. My body burst into flame, and I felt my human shell disintegrate. I was my true self once more. A look of utter satisfaction crossed the old woman's face, and I saw peace replace her pain. Then she was gone. Darkness filled my prison. I was alone.

And here I have stayed. Hatred and rage consume me. I strain at my bonds, but they do not give. I am trapped, just as I had been trapped for so many thousands of years. For a long time, I struggle. Then I settle down. I have escaped before. I will escape again.

I begin to chip at my fetters. Sooner or later, they will weaken and break. I will find another soul to take, and once again I will walk the earth. I have time. I have all the time in the world.

The End

The Cursed Stag

Nils Visser

Patcham, Sussex, 250 AD

PROLOGUS

The dark, moist earth gave way readily when the man clawed at it with his bare hands.

It was dark. The man hadn't dared to bring a lit torch, but the full moon illuminated his frantic digging. He was in a hurry, had to be back before he was missed. Nonetheless, every now and then he would pause to glance at the object next to him. A bronze statuette gleaming in the moonlight, depicting perfectly the regal bearing of an antlered stag. It was valuable and a means to an end: A future as a free man.

The digger tugged at his slave collar, then cursed when he heard someone call his name. He knew who it was. He groaned when he realised he was going to need another, much larger hole in the earth.

I.

Flavia and Lucia were identical twins, although it had been ten years since one had been mistaken for the other.

They were the property of Marcus Valerius Gallus. They were assets of his villa, a large complex in one of the many broad valleys between the great domed hills along the south-eastern coastline of Britannia.

Flavia lived in the *pars rustica* at the lower end of the villa, together with the other house slaves and livestock. Lucia lived further away, out of sight, behind a low ridge where the field slaves were penned into small huts at night. Their master occasionally allowed Flavia to visit her sister when she had pleased him.

The field slave huts, simple thatched rectangular structures of wattle and daub, were enclosed by a palisade. Flavia greeted the guards at the gate and then made straight for the hut which Lucia shared with nine others. Their ten rickety cots took up most of the space inside.

As always, Flavia and Lucia fell into each other's arms for a long hug. The others in the hut left to grant the sisters privacy. Not out of consideration for Lucia, but as recognition of Flavia's higher status as a house slave.

For Lucia these visits were the only moments of brightness in an otherwise miserable existence. Her sister was the only person who wasn't disgusted by Lucia's disfigured face. Flavia didn't even seem to notice the mangled scar tissue that marred most of Lucia's left cheek, nor the gaping hole where a nostril had been torn away.

"I haven't got long," Flavia said, after they had disentangled from their embrace.

Lucia nodded. "I haven't got any news. Other than that, old Tiro is on the mend, he'll live to work another harvest."

Much of their talk during these visits involved the exchange of gossip. Sometimes they also passed messages along. Being a conduit of news gave Lucia her only standing in the pens.

In general, Lucia's news mostly concerned illness, punishment, and death. Flavia, on the other hand, usually had far more to tell, not just tidings from the *pars rustica,* but also the comings and goings in the luxurious master residence called *pars urbana.*

"Half the household has been packing," Flavia told Lucia. "Dominus and Domina leave tomorrow, to their townhouse in Regnum (Chichester)"

"When the cat's asleep," Lucia quipped.

"There won't be much rejoicing by mice," Flavia said with a wry smile. "You know well enough *Major Domus* and *Villicus* will run household and estate with a tight hand."

Flavia continued to pass on further gossip. Lucia tried to focus, for the others would ask her later, but found it hard to concentrate.

She kept on gazing at her sister. At twenty-four they were getting old. Neither of the twins expected to live beyond thirty. Lucia looked permanently pale and haggard and her body was worn by continuous heavy labour, but age hadn't made much of an impact on Flavia yet. The twins were of a slender build, with light skin, blue eyes, and fair hair. That, combined with Flavia's youthful grace, meant that she remained one of Dominus's favourite bed-slaves.

Lucia never tired of looking at her sister. The sight of Flavia filled her with wonder. It was like looking into one of Domina's polished mirrors and seeing herself without the monstrous scars...seeing what might have been.

That could have been me.

Flavia had finished talking and was looking at Lucia expectantly, clearly waiting for some response. Lucia wasn't sure what, the last words she had registered were about something the cook had gotten up to with a laundry girl in the posticum (servant and house-slave entrance) of the *pars urbana.*

"Cook's a fool," Lucia ventured. Flavia nodded. "It'll all go wrong faster than you can cook asparagus, mark my words."

Lucia changed the subject. "How long will Dominus and Domina be gone?"

"Three, four weeks? Why?"

"Matralia. They'll be in Regnum for Matralia."

Understanding lit up Flavia's face. Matralia, Festival of Mothers, was celebrated in honour of Mater Matuta, Goddess of childbirth, puberty, and motherhood. Free-born mothers were honoured by their children and husbands on this day. Special cakes were baked in earthenware pots and offered to the Goddess in a ceremony attended by married women only, barring one slave who would be ritually humiliated and beaten bloody in honour of the Goddess and motherhood.

It was clever of Lucia to connect the visit to Regnum with Matralia. It hadn't been mentioned yet in the *pars rustica.* Flavia looked forward to breaking the news that it would be some poor soul in Regnum who would feel the lashes this year, not one of their own.

Flavia knew that of the two of them Lucia was the thinker. It wasn't the first time that Lucia had offered insight into life at the villa proper, even though Lucia was a persona non grata there and hadn't set foot in the villa for a decade. Lucia was even excluded from the Saturnalia celebrations, when Dominus and Domina offered all their slaves a banquet in the main courtyard. Yet somehow Lucia managed to understand things that eluded Flavia.

Time was running out. Flavia was secretly grateful. Looking at Lucia's face was hard. For her sister's sake, Flavia pretended not to notice, but she was all too aware of those horrific scars. She sometimes had nightmares about waking up to discover that her face had been changed into that twisted and mangled mirror image presented by Lucia.

That could have been me.

*That **SHOULD** have been me.*

It wasn't so much the ruination of Lucia's face that caused Flavia distress. Instead, it was the reminder of who had caused it...raking her heart with sharp claws of remorse.

*...My fault...MY fault...**MY** fault.*

II.

Marcus Valerius Gallus sat behind his desk in the tablinum (office). It was one of the central rooms at the southern face of the main wing of the villa. That allowed Gallus oversight of much of the *pars urbana,* and he could also step outside onto the portico for a view of the greater part of his estate. Looking out over the fields which his family had owned for generations always instilled him with a sense of pride and duty.

The villa was busy, preparing for the transfer to the town house. Gallus ignored the preparations, focusing instead on the letter he had received from Regnum. It was from the chief municipal magistrate, inviting Gallus to supply the slave for the city's Matralia celebration.

Gallus had already confirmed, for it would see the name of Marcus Valerius Gallus elevated to the attention of important provincial officials. The decision that Gallus had yet to make was which slave to yield up for the celebration.

He stood up and turned to an alcove in the wall behind his desk. It held one of his prized possessions, a bronze statuette of a stag. He stroked its back, enjoying the feel of the smooth, cool metal beneath his fingers.

Gallus could sense the discomfort of his two attendant slaves. He knew that the house and field slaves considered the statuette cursed. A learned man like Gallus scoffed at such simple superstitions of the ignorant. The stag was pleasing to the eye, but it was just a representation of the woodland god Sylvanus. Nonetheless, Gallus didn't discourage his slaves from believing it to be cursed. The more they feared the better.

It struck Gallus that he was no nearer to coming to a decision and he scolded himself for letting his thoughts stray. He lived his life by certain simple principles. The first was that nothing came from nothing. Success required hard work, dedication, and commitment. The second was *Vivamus, Moriendum Est*, a reminder that the inevitability of death invited indulgence in pleasure while it was still possible.

Gallus had divided his waking hours accordingly. When he rose in the morning, he ran his estate as efficiently as he could to increase his already considerable wealth. At the end of the day, when twilight set in, Gallus allowed the emergence of his alter-ego, whose maxim was *Carpe Noctum*: Seize the Night.

Gallus sighed. The great poet Ovid had been right when he wrote that there is no such thing as pure pleasure because it is always accompanied by some anxiety.

He walked out onto the portico. The situation wasn't one that should have left him indecisive. There were plenty of other matters that required his attention. Last minute arrangements with *Villicus* regarding the management of the estate, for one. Gallus also wanted to be prepared for Regnum, where he would likely be asked for his opinion on troubling issues, such as the continued political turmoil in the empire. On a more local level there were Saxon pirates. Those barbarians had been raiding the Cantii coast. He glanced down the valley. Although not visible, the sea wasn't far away. The villa was within striking distance. How long before the Saxons extended their range to include the Regni coast? Increased protection would require extra taxation, a matter that would be fiercely debated in Regnum.

Gallus spotted Flavia walking back to the villa. He recalled that he had given her permission to visit her hideous sibling.

Flavia was part of his Matralia deliberations. In contrast to smaller domestic ceremonies, the ritual in Regnum would take place in one of the city's larger temples. The slave might well die, chased around the temple by scores of free-born matrons eager to land blows and draw blood to ensure good health for their families.

A slave's death was a small price to pay for the favour of Mater Matuta and improved social standing – but which one to sacrifice?

Gallus should have sent Flavia to the pens long ago. Perhaps the time had come. That would also allow him to rid the estate of the dour presence of Flavia's monstrous twin. *Villicus* ensured that Lucia was assigned work out of Gallus's sight, but just knowing the hideous creature was near was offensive.

The other option was the Frisian girl. When Gallus had purchased her at auction in Portus Novus (Portslade) not long ago, he'd had high hopes. He had been mesmerised by her pretty, innocent face, golden hair, and willowy limbs. The Frisian was intended as a replacement for Flavia, but the girl was useless for copulation. She just lay there, lifeless like a sack of grain. As for other tasks in the household, when she wasn't curled up in a corner weeping incessantly, her tear-stained face exuded misery. The girl had been given several whippings already to enforce more cheer, but it hadn't helped.

"Hopeless," Gallus muttered to himself.

"What is hopeless, Husband?" His wife Tullia joined him on the portico. She glanced at the letter Gallus held in his hand. "Have you made a decision?"

"In a manner of speaking." It was but a small matter. Delaying the decision would allow him to focus on more important issues. "We'll take both Flavia and the Frisian to Regnum and decide there."

"Very well," Tullia said. "I'll tell *Major Domus*."

III.

Lucia and some of the others had been ordered to dig a new latrine trench for the pens. The men dug, and the women carried away baskets full of excavated earth to fill up the old trench. It was a warm summer's day, the old latrine smelled foul and was buzzing with flies.

It had taken Lucia a few days to find out Flavia had been taken to Regnum. She wasn't surprised that Flavia hadn't been allowed to say goodbye. Slaves were objects, devoid of personality, human emotions, and emotive needs.

Lucia was worried. Flavia had never been taken on previous trips to Regnum. Why had she been chosen now? Lucia hoped fervently that it wasn't related to Matralia.

Lucia approached the old trench and knelt at its edge to empty her basket. To do so standing up would have resulted in the foul muck below splashing up. She rose to her feet, grimacing at the pain in her right knee and lower back. It was getting worse, but she mustn't tarry because the foreman was quick to lash out with his whip. She made her way back to the new trench, losing herself in thought again.

Both she and Flavia had been named by Dominus. They had been enslaved so young that they didn't know their birth names. They were Cimbrian, from across the Saxon Sea, but had no recollection of family or native language. They only had each other.

As twins, they had been presented as a single novelty lot at auction in Novus Portus. Dominus hadn't hesitated to outbid other interested parties. He had sent them to the *pars rustica* and paid them no further attention for years. His interest had been rekindled when they had started to become women. *Major Domus* had informed them that they would soon be summoned to the master's cubiculum one night, both at the same time. The twins were frightened but it was something of a relief that they would be together. Fate, however, was to intervene...

IV.

In the Regnum townhouse, Gallus decided to send the Frisian to the temple for Matralia. She died of her injuries a few days afterwards and none mourned her passing.

V.

It would be weeks before Flavia earned a visit to the pens after returning from Regnum.

"Dominus bought new slaves," Flavia apologised to Lucia after their customary hug. "Including a rebellious red-head from Hibernia. He's been breaking her in."

"It matters not." Lucia smiled and took both of Flavia's hands into her own. "Tell me about Regnum. What was it like? You look well, sister."

It was true; there was a rosy glow to Flavia which Lucia couldn't place. It soon became apparent why. Although much impressed by her first trip to a city, Flavia mostly wanted to talk about another matter. One of the other new slaves called Terrax.

"He's from the south somewhere," Flavia told Lucia. "With jet black hair, a smile to die for, and eyes...oh his eyes!"

Lucia was cautious, especially when she gathered that this Terrax seemed equally interested in Flavia. Her sister and this man contrived short meetings in various corners of the villa to exchange sweet talk.

"Flavia." Lucia shook her head. "Be careful. Do be careful."

Senior slaves, those who had served Dominus for a long time, were permitted to marry and start a family. Dominus would never allow it for one of his bed-slaves. At most, he would offer them as a reward to senior slaves or free-born servants after he grew tired of them.

"Of course, we are careful," Flavia assured her sister. "Nothing has happened." *Yet!* Lucia wasn't reassured.

"If Dominus finds out..."

"Why must you always be so glum," Flavia complained. "Just because you will never..." She stopped, blushed.

"Will never what?"

"Never mind," Flavia mumbled. "I just hoped that you would be...could be...pleased for me."

"I am, it's just that..."

It went on like that, the conversation stuck in a loop. Mutual frustration arose, but they tried to part on good terms.

The twins would never see each other again in this world.

VI.

Terrax was a clever man, but that was also his weakness. He reckoned himself cleverer than all around him and liked to play with people as if he were directing actors on a stage.

Born a free man, he had gambled away more than he earned as a lowly scribe. He had been enslaved as payment for his debts. As a scribe he was treated better than most slaves, but he yearned for freedom. His plan was to secure enough funds and go far, far away. Perhaps as far as Africa or Anatolia, then set himself up as a scribe and make a modest living. As a free man.

Terrax wasted no time in exploring the potentials of his new master's villa. He was fascinated when he heard reports of the cursed stag. Of course, his new Dominus had more valuable statuettes of deities, but a man could only carry so many. There were those in Londinium, purveyors of the occult, who would pay well for a cursed object.

A plan began to form. Befriending Flavia had been easy. He had chosen her because she didn't seem to have close relations with anyone in the *pars rustica*. She had a relative of sorts in the pens but had remained vague about the precise nature of that relation, so Terrax assumed it wasn't that important.

Flavia played an important part in his plans. Not only would she help gain him entry to the *pars urbana*, she would also accompany him to Londinium as loot walking on her own two feet. Terrax intended to sell her once they had reached the great city. There were brothels enough where they didn't ask too many questions if the girl was pretty.

VII.

Flavia waited until Dominus started snoring and then slipped out of his bed. She donned her tunic and stepped out of the cubiculum. Cato, one of Dominus's attendants, was waiting to walk her to the posticum and let her out of the *pars urbana*.

Flavia and Cato had done this often over the last decade. They rarely spoke because the household was asleep, but Flavia had always found Cato a comforting presence.

The splendour of the mosaic floors and frescoed walls was barely visible in the dim light of the occasional oil lamp, but Flavia's ears told her Cato's slight limp was more pronounced than usual, and his breathing troubled.

"Your ailment?" Flavia whispered. Cato nodded. They reached the posticum.

"I'll see myself out, Cato," Flavia said. "You get yourself some rest if you can."

"Are you sure?"

Flavia nodded. The posticum door had a latch that would fall into a locked position when she closed it behind her.

She could hear Cato's irregular footfall fade away as she walked down the corridor to the door.

Flavia opened the door and nearly screamed in fright when a shadow rushed in from the night, pressing her against the wall, placing a hand over her mouth.

A hoarse whisper: "It's me. Terrax. Don't make a noise."

Wide-eyed, Flavia nodded. Terrax removed his hand from her mouth and stepped away from her.

"You aren't supposed to be here." Flavia whispered. "If *Villicus*..."

"Dead drunk." Terrax grinned. "Probably passed out already. Wouldn't notice it if Hannibal crashed an elephant through the main gate."

Flavia stared at him. She was torn between her fierce feelings for him on the one hand, and the risk of this meeting on the other.

"Terrax, what are...?"

"Hush, my Love. I'll explain later."

Flavia shook her head, small pangs of worry and fear competing with the butterflies his nearness evoked in her belly.

"You need to trust me." Terrax took her in his arms. "Go back to your dormitory and pretend nothing has happened. I will follow soon."

"Soon? What..."

He caressed her cheek. "I'm ensuring our future, my Love."

"No, Terrax. No."

"We'll leave this hellhole. Go somewhere far away. Start a new life. Just you and I. Together. Don't you want that? I want to be with you more than anything."

Flavia stared at him aghast. Her memory supplied dreadful scenes from the past. The howling of ferocious dogs brought by slave hunters. Battered and bleeding runaways returned. The collective unease as all slaves were assembled to witness punishment. Chilling screams...screams that turned into exhausted moans. Mewls, whimpers, sighs...and at long last silence.

"No," Flavia said. "Terrax, not like this. Come back to the *rustica* with me. Now."

A flicker of irritation flashed across his face. His voice became harsher. "You'll do as I say, Flavia, if you want us to be together. You go back, now. Make no mention of this." He pushed her out of their embrace. Numbed by his sudden coldness, Flavia nodded silently. He indicated the door. She opened it quietly and stepped out as Terrax prowled down the posticum.

Flavia didn't return to her dormitory though. She hid behind some carts in the courtyard instead, to keep an eye on the posticum door.

An eternity seemed to pass by before Terrax emerged, cradling an object. It was mostly wrapped in a rag, but its exposed parts caught the moonlight. Flavia recognised the upraised head and antlers instantly. Her heart skipped a beat, and an icy tingle traversed the length of her spine...

VIII.

The girls were on their knees in the tablinum, scrubbing the floor. Although Lucia tried to hide her fear, Flavia knew that she dreaded the expected summons to attend to Dominus in his cubiculum.

Flavia wasn't looking forward to it either, but she could also see positive sides and tried to cheer her sister up.

"We shall become his favourites," Flavia said softly, for they weren't supposed to talk during work. "You know how well he treated Sabina."

"I know what happened to Sabina when he grew bored of her," Lucia countered.

"Sabina was too dull to hold his attention. We're different." Lucia shrugged.

"Oh Lucia! We'll be fed the best of Cook's treats, dressed in the finest tunics. No more scrubbing floors for us. Maybe Dominus will even buy us gifts."

Her eye fell upon the bronze stag raising its antlered head. Forgetting all caution, Flavia jumped up and made to the alcove. "Just imagine..."

She stroked the stag's smooth back. "...owning something valuable! Treasures such as this."

"Flavia," Lucia hissed. "Get down. You'll get us into trouble."

Flavia gave the stag a last pat and then rejoined Lucia on the floor. Seconds later Dominus stormed into the tablinum, red with anger ...

IX.

In a temporary lapse of daytime discipline, Gallus delayed a task to linger in the *pars urbanus*. He observed the twins on their knees in his office, considering his intended conquest of their sweet young bodies. He would send for them this very night.

Anticipation transformed into astonishment, then outrage, when one of the girls deserted her duties and started pawing the bronze statuette.

Gallus strode into the tablinum. "HOW DARE YOU?" he thundered. "How dare you lay your filthy slave hands on my possessions?" He grabbed the nearest twin by her hair, and dragged the struggling, whimpering girl across the floor to the alcove. The other one screamed but Gallus ignored her, rage dictating his actions.

He picked up the statuette with his free hand. "I'll give you a closer look, impertinent slave." He used all his strength to thrust the girl's face and the statuette together. The girl screamed. Her sister did too. Gallus bellowed as he rubbed the slave's face against the statuette.

"YOU DO **NOT** TOUCH **MY** POSSESSIONS. DO YOU UNDERSTAND?"

Gallus felt warm liquid splashing on his sandaled feet. He looked down, frowning, then yanked the slave's hair to raise her face. It was a gory mess. Her nose had been ripped open; her cheek shredded to reveal startlingly white bone. He had forgotten about the antlers.

X.

Flavia shuddered at the memories. Lucia had forgiven her, but Flavia would never forgive herself.

Terrax was making his way to a small side door in the courtyard. It should have been locked, but it wasn't and Terrax slipped through it like a thief in the night.

Flavia shut her eyes, reliving that horrible day. *Major Domus* had arranged for Lucia to be taken to the villa's physician. Flavia had wanted to follow, but Dominus had grabbed her arm, angry still.

"Your sister's stupidity has cost me a good slave," he had snarled.

Flavia had trembled with fright, not daring to confess the truth in case it triggered a new explosion of fury.

He had shrugged. "If she lives, I'll sell her to the mines." Flavia had begged him not to.

Dominus had made a proposal. He would refrain from selling Lucia to the mines for as long as Flavia managed to please him. She would have to learn how to make him feel like a God amongst men. She had done so, anything to spare her stricken sister further anguish.

A surge of anger at Terrax spurred Flavia to follow him. Terrax didn't know that Dominus would immediately suspect the twins when he discovered the stag gone. Flavia wouldn't, couldn't, have the statuette inflict further suffering on Lucia.

Once out of the villa, she saw Terrax making his way down the sloping fields, towards the small river that meandered through the valley. He squatted at the very edge of the lowest field and began to dig into the earth.

Flavia's determination grew as she approached Terrax. She would make him return the statuette before its absence, or theirs for that matter, was discovered. There simply wasn't another option.

"Terrax," she called out softly as she came closer. "Terrax."

XI.

Dominus sent Terrax on an errand the next day, to pass a message to *Villicus*, who was supervising the construction of a ditch in the top fields.

It was a relief to be away from the villa, abuzz with rumours concerning Flavia's disappearance.

As Terrax approached, one of the slaves came scrambling out of the ditch and caused him to stop in his tracks. Her face was pale and haggard, her hair listless, skin and tunic covered in bits of earth as if she had risen from the grave. Flavia's countenance was completed by horrendous scars there where he had raked her face open with the only weapon he had to hand the previous night: the bronze stag.

This before he had brought the stag's rump down repeatedly to stave in her skull. She'd been dead. He'd buried her. Yet here she was.

Terrax wet himself and began to scream.

XII.

"We are holding a wolf by its ears," Gallus growled at his wife. "Have you seen the effect she has on Terrax?"

"I have, Husband," Tullia answered. "It's sorcery, there is no other explanation. The man will never be in his right mind again."

"She must be punished."

Tullia inclined her head in agreement. "But you cannot end a slave's life without justification."

"This is where the little Frisian was worth something after all. I can now appeal to dignitaries from Portus Novus and Regnum to bear witness."

"Sorcery is hard to prove," Tullia warned.

"The cause of fear is ignorance, is what learned men will say," Gallus agreed.

"Then again, if they see how Terrax responds to Lucia..."

"Not only that. Once they hear how Lucia aided and abetted the escape of her sister..."

"Indeed." Tullia said. "That will earn her immediate condemnation. Slaves must be kept in place, but..."

"But what?"

"How will you prevent Lucia rising from the dead? I don't want her malignant spirit to wander amongst the living."

"Leave that up to me."

XIII.

Lucia's mind was a confused daze. She had been seized and thrust into a dark cell for a reason she couldn't fathom. None bothered to tell her, though one of the guards did mention that Flavia had run away.

It was hard to believe that Flavia would have done so without confiding in her sister. Lucia alternated between hope that Flavia was by now far away and safe, and fear that something more sinister was at play.

Weeks passed before she was dragged out into bright daylight, to be escorted by guards to the very edge of the estate. All the slaves were there, as were Dominus and Domina, as well as three Roman dignitaries.

There was a curiously long grave, at one end of which lay a broad wooden beam. There was no sign of a cross arm, the tell-tale sign of crucifixion, but Lucia didn't doubt that her last moments on this cruel earth would be painful.

As a slave, she wasn't entitled to a trial. Nor was any explanation offered. At a signal from Dominus, the guards stripped her and threw her on the ground, to begin lashing her with their whips until Lucia's back was bloody and raw, her initial screams faded into desperate sobs.

When the whipping was finally over, she was hauled onto her feet, barely able to stand on her legs, barely able to think straight.

Two guards paraded a man into view. The one whose strange reaction had triggered this fresh new hell. Lucia suspected he was Terrax, but it was difficult to imagine that this pathetic wreck of a man had made such an impression on Flavia.

He started to tremble when he saw Lucia and pointed a shaking finger at her. "You...! You...!"

Lucia numbly shook her head. She had never met him before, yet he was staring at her as if he were seeing a...

Realisation dawned, accompanied by a stream of high-pitched gibberish from Terrax, who attempted to back away but was restrained by the guards.

Utter hopelessness swept through Lucia. She was sure now that Flavia was gone from this life. She stared dully as one of the guards slit Terrax's throat and then tumbled the dying man into the far end of the long grave. She didn't struggle when they forcibly laid her on the beam, nor scream when her bloodied back made contact with the rough wood.

Her arms were pressed against either side of the beam and held there. One of the guards produced a hammer and long nails. She felt the tip of the nail pressed against one of her wrists. Saw the hammer rise...

Lucia shut her eyes tightly. The pain was excruciating, but distant somehow. When Lucia opened her eyes, she was surprised to be looking down at herself...her broken, bloodied body writhing and twisting on the beam as more nails were driven through her body...her other wrist, her ankles, knees...Copious blood mixed with the earth around the beam to form gory mud.

That other, the bloodied thing below, screamed, but not in pain this time. Instead, she uttered a stream of curses. She cursed Dominus. She cursed Domina. She cursed their children. She cursed all Romans and swore her spirit wouldn't rest until their provinces on Britannia were destroyed, their mighty cities and precious villas reduced to smoking rubble, inhabitants dead or enslaved, their roads choked by weeds.

The curses ceased when they flipped the beam, forcing Lucia's face and body into the gory mud. A nail was being driven into the wood behind her head. Each hammer blow caused an explosion of noise, but Lucia barely registered the nail being driven deeper into the wood, its sharp end nearing her skull.

All pain seemed gone now, reduced to dull throbs. The hatred was gone, all spewed out. The witnesses of her punishment faded from her view, to be replaced by Flavia's beautiful face, a sight that filled Lucia with love. Her last conscious thought, as the nail was driven into her skull, was that they would be together again.

The beam was tossed into the grave, where it landed on its side, after which it was filled in with dark, moist earth.

POST SCRIPTUM

Lucia and Terrax were discovered in June 1936 by workmen digging ditches in Patcham...a long nail still embedded in Lucia's skull. The remains are currently on display in Brighton Museum. The stag statuette is also there to see...for those who dare.

The End

Quake

P.J. Blakey-Novis

At school, I distinctly remember being taught the Earth sciences. My interest in these things only grew stronger into adulthood. I genuinely found it fascinating, impressive even. Volcanoes, earthquakes, tsunamis, and tornadoes, all with their immense power and potential to cause catastrophes on an unthinkable scale. I missed the opportunity to go to a regular university as I had already left home and needed to be working in order to support myself, but once I reached my early twenties, I decided to take up studying again, part-time. I completed a degree in Earth Sciences, which I passed with a decent grade, and naively thought I'd be able to walk into a position that I had always dreamed of. For the first six months I couldn't even find a relevant job to apply for. When I eventually did find something which sounded ideal, I could not get past the first stage of the interview due to lack of experience. Stupid bloody Catch-22; need the job to gain experience, need experience to get the job. And from then on, for the last fifteen years, experiencing a natural disaster personally has only been a dream.

A lot of people would say that it is a strange dream to have, to want to be caught up in that kind of tragedy, and it is hard for me to explain the desire. I suppose it's similar to those guys who chase tornadoes across America, getting as close as possible to them, risking their lives for that adrenalin rush. I never thought I'd have the chance to realise this dream, living in the UK where disasters on this scale simply didn't happen, and not having the resources to travel anywhere that they did occur. The closest I had got to experiencing an earthquake at that time was at The Natural History Museum in London, where they have an 'earthquake room' which is supposed to simulate the 7.2 magnitude earthquake which hit Kobe in the winter of 1995. This all changed six months ago.

I'd never had much in the way of family. There were a number of people who I knew were related to me, but I had left my hometown at a young age and had very little contact with any of them. Even at Christmas, I only received perhaps two or three cards from family members, and I certainly never visited any of them. Which is why a letter from an aunt came as a surprise. The name, Martha, only rang a vague bell in my mind and I could not recall ever seeing this person, or what she looked like. The letter explained that she had contacted my mother to request my address, and that her sister, another of my aunts, had passed away. I had no real feeling about this, as I did not know the woman. However, the now deceased Aunt Beryl had apparently been rather fond of me.

I don't know how Beryl's will had been split among the family, and what percentage my inheritance made up, but £15000 was a very welcome surprise. I contacted Aunt Martha by telephone, trying to sound saddened by the news of Beryl's passing, talked a little about myself and what I'd been doing for the last twenty or so years since we had seen one another. Martha told me that she had not wanted to send a cheque, in case it was lost in the post, so took my bank details in order to make a transfer. The money was in my account within two hours of ending our conversation.

The rest of the day passed in a blur of research and planning. I was well aware that most earthquakes occur around what has been dubbed The Ring of Fire, incorporating New Zealand, The Philippines, Japan, and the western coasts of North and South America. My first thought had been to travel to Japan, but the visa would be restrictive and there was no guarantee I would experience an earthquake in the thirty days I was permitted to stay. It was as I looked into travelling to the Philippines that I came across the perfect solution - charity work. The company would arrange the visas, provide food and accommodation, and collect me from the airport. I only needed to make my way to Manila International Airport and make a charitable donation of £2000, then I could stay on for as long as I wished.

I took to the change well; I enjoyed the company of the other charity workers, loved working outdoors in the warmth, and took pride in the help we were providing for the local people. Over the first three months we experienced six minor earthquakes. They all scored low on the Richter Scale, and did very little damage, but the thrill was incredible. As soon as the first tremor could be felt, a rush of adrenalin hit me and I hoped, more than anything, that this would be a big one. There were no large earthquakes in the Philippines for the first five months of my visit but then it came. Although I felt the tremors, the epicentre was almost 100 miles away. We had no television in the camp, relying on the radio for news. The quake had not been as severe as the one in Kobe in 1995 but was not far off. The news reports described the carnage left behind, the death toll steadily rising into the thousands. This was what I had been waiting for, and I knew I could not keep away. Under the guise of wanting to see if I could help, I arranged transport to the site of the most destruction and was there less than twenty-four hours after the earthquake had struck.

Two of the other men from camp had offered to join me, and despite wanting to travel alone, I could think of no justification for turning down their help. The closest the rickety old bus could take us was a little over a mile from where the real damage had occurred, so the three of us made the rest of the journey on foot. Twenty minutes of walking, and we could smell the death in the air; that distinctive, metallic odour of spilled blood, a grim hint of flesh already beginning to decompose in the heat, and a sickening, burned smell. The emergency services were on the scene, gathered around fallen buildings, rescue dogs barking into dark corners of the destruction to announce the site of someone trapped.

My two associates from camp had already joined the team of rescuers in pulling at broken bricks and bent steel cables, desperate to get to the faint sound of the sobbing which came from within. I took the opportunity to slip away unnoticed, keen to explore the area of ground which had opened up so violently. There was an unmissable increase in the level of damage as I made my way towards the centre of what had been the town. I could see no buildings which remained intact, not even the Catholic church had survived this act of God. The whole scene appeared post-apocalyptic; as though humanity was on the verge of extinction, as if the entire globe now looked this way.

The streets were littered with rubble, and I had to take care as I made my way across the debris. At one point, I looked away from the ground and my foot made contact with something soft, in contrast to the bricks I had been walking across. I heard a wet sound and looked down, only to find I had trodden on what appeared to be the front half of a dog. I felt nothing for that poor creature, only a pull to find the place where the ground had opened; it was as though I was being called to it.

It had taken me thirty minutes to find my way to the edge of what was now a large crevice in the ground. I had counted no less than twenty-four dead bodies on my journey. At least, I presumed them to be dead judging by the amount of blood and impossible positioning of the limbs. I did not take the time to check them, and that makes me sound like a monster. The opening in the ground was not wide, less than a couple of feet, but its length seemed to continue for as far as I could see. The few rescue workers dotted about were too preoccupied with the injured to pay any attention to this strange westerner who was staring into the abyss.

There was no way of seeing how deep the crack was, but everything that I had studied suggested that earthquake cracks, even ones of this magnitude, were rarely more than a few feet deep. The way I saw it, that would be shallow enough to easily pull myself out of again, but I had to feel what it was like to be in there. Nervously, I glanced around to check that I wasn't being watched. Everyone was still absorbed in the rescue efforts, so I moved myself into a sitting position, legs hanging into the opening. As subtly as I could manage, I lowered myself in, my feet feeling their way down the muddy interior until they found an area solid enough to stand on.

I was in the hole up to my shoulders, so even at this end of the crevice the depth must have been around five feet. I suddenly realised how ridiculous I must look to those on the surface, just a head visible above the ground, and instinctively ducked out of sight. Although I had never read this as being fact, it seemed logical to me that the crack would get deeper towards the middle, before shallowing out again towards the other end. I did not know how long the crack went on for, but finding myself inside of it was exhilarating, and I shuffled myself along further.

There was an increase in depth, but only another couple of feet. I found myself enclosed, entombed perhaps, between two seven-foot walls of earth, but I was not afraid. I knew I could go back to where I had entered the ground and would be able to pull myself out. I have no way of knowing how long I was down there, but I recall making the decision to return to where I had started. That is when the second quake hit.

I can remember the tremors as the earth beneath my feet shifted, the sudden darkness as the loose ground above tumbled viciously on to me, and then only blackness. In hindsight, I should have expected it; most large earthquakes are followed soon after by a series of smaller ones, but the thought had never entered my head. When I came to, I found myself in total darkness, but able to move. My head hurt, as though it had been struck by something heavy, but the rest of my body seemed surprisingly unscathed. Moving my head in all directions, I could not find a single point at which light was able to penetrate the darkness and panic began to set it.

I knew I could not be far beneath the surface and reached up with the idiotic hope that I could simply push the overlaying earth away and call for help. Nothing budged, even a tiny amount, and my efforts only led to me getting a mouthful of damp mud as the loose soil tumbled down on to my face. I had no torch, of course, and no phone to use as a flashlight. I pressed the button on the side of my watch, hoping its meagre illumination would be of some assistance, but it did not respond. I ran my hand over its face and felt the crack in it, confirmation that the watch had not survived.

Sound does not travel well through the earth so, when the singing began, I thought someone on the surface had managed to create an opening. The sound became louder, a beautifully haunting sound which brought images of sailors and mermaids to my mind, but still no hint of light came with it. I sat there for an immeasurable amount of time, listening to what were unmistakably songs of some kind, strangely content at that moment. The trauma of my situation, the music, or quite probably both, sent me into a deep, yet fitful, sleep.

There was no alteration in the impenetrable darkness when I finally awoke, yet I knew that I was somewhere else. The air smelled different, cleaner perhaps. The singing persisted but more quietly; not further away, just not as loud as it had first been. The total lack of light, and therefore complete redundancy of my eyes, had heightened my other senses - in particular, my hearing. Now, the singing was not the only sound I could make out, but other noises alongside it. Scurrying, scraping, scratching.

"Who's there?" I called out in barely more than a whisper. My throat felt dry from a lack of water, and I had not uttered a word for what I presumed was many hours. There came no reply, but I knew I was not alone in these depths beneath the surface. I reached out my arms as far as they would go from my sitting position and felt nothing. I managed to pull myself to my feet, standing slowly for fear of hitting my head again. I reached full height without striking the earth above me. I reached my arms up, tiptoeing, and could feel nothing. Wherever I now was, it was much larger than when I had fallen asleep.

"Who's singing?" I asked. Still no reply. Beginning to get frustrated with the lack of response, and with a more rational fear setting in, I started to scream for help. Looking back, this should have been my very first response; at least then I knew I was close to the surface. Now, in this place, it felt deeper...much deeper. I managed to release the word *help* four times before something struck me in the chest, knocking me to the floor. The singing had stopped, and I found myself lying on my back with a weight on top of me.

Frozen, in both fear and surprise, I remained still and waited. My head involuntarily twitched to the side as I felt something graze my right ear. *A worm,* I thought. It had certainly felt like a worm, cold and slimy to the touch, but as more and more of these 'worms' touched the side of my face I knew they must be something else. I could feel them tracing lines down my cheeks, parallel with one another, five lines on each side. *Not worms, fingers!* I realised, pulling myself back as far as I could manage.

I was still being straddled by the owner of these worm-like appendages, and so I placed a hand on either side of the creature's waist and pushed it to one side. I managed to pull myself up to a standing position, heart racing, sweat pouring from my brow. I could see nothing but could sense movement in front of me. I wanted to scream for help, but that had angered my attacker before, and I was too terrified to do anything other than wait.

I felt the slimy parts touching my hands, feeling strangely like hands themselves; almost human in size but with unmistakable webbing between the fingers. I could feel the creature's breath on my throat, suggesting it was a few inches shorter than me. More than anything, at that moment, I wanted to be able to see - to see what stood before me, to try to work out where I was, to find a way to escape. My curiosity, my obsession, had led me to this place and there was little doubt that this would become my grave.

The webbed hands ran all over my body as I stood completely still. When the inspection was complete, I heard damp footsteps as the creature moved away and resumed the singing. A dizziness came over me at the sound and I sat, soon falling again into a deep sleep.

When I awoke, the light hurt my eyes to the point that I could not fully open them for several minutes. It was a shock to the system, following the intense darkness I had found myself in and, when I did manage to focus on my surroundings, I knew I was no longer with the earth. The light filled the room, emanating from electric strip lights, made all the more intense by the clinical white of the room I found myself in.

I was in a bed, buried beneath a thick white duvet. In fact, everything in the room was white. I ached all over but could not be seriously injured as there were no tubes attached to my body, no machines beeping gently beside me, only silence. I cautiously lifted the covers to find that I was wearing a standard issue hospital gown. It was impossible to say how long I had been there, but I could not recall anything following my inspection by that vile creature. I hoped that I had merely slept for a matter of hours, but I was soon to learn that was far from the truth.

Sitting upright caused a wave of nausea to hit me, along with a dizziness that almost brought me tumbling from the side of the bed. I held the position, somewhere between horizontal and vertical, until the feeling passed enough for me to swing my legs toward the cold floor. There was too little sensation in my feet, a strange mix of pins and needles and numbness, and as I edged off the bed my legs gave way. I managed to place my hands out in front of me to break the fall a little, but my knees took a hard knock and I felt a strange, wet sensation in my abdomen.

Rolling myself over, I swung my almost useless legs out in front of me and used my hands to pull myself back so that I was able to rest against the spotless wall. The brilliantly white gown now showed a spreading crimson stain, and, in a panic, I lifted my gown to inspect the area. An inch or so beneath my navel was a line of stitches around six inches across. My movements had caused it to split at one end, and the blood now flowed freely. I watched in horror as the red liquid ran down between my legs and began to form a pool on the floor.

Frantically, my eyes darted around the room in search of a button to press which would summon the medical staff. I could find no button, no way of contacting anyone, so used my arms to crawl across the floor to the only door in the room, a trail of blood marking my path. I reached the door, but it took all my strength to pull myself up by the handle, only to find it locked. I bashed my fists against it until my hands were red, but no one came to my aid, and I could hear no sounds from beyond the locked door. The blood loss, combined with the exertion, caused me to lose consciousness, slumped against the door.

I was brought around by the door being pushed against me. I let out a quiet 'help', trying to roll myself away far enough for the door to be opened, far enough for someone to gain access and do something about this seemingly infinite supply of blood I was losing. My head felt light, and I had no doubt that I was close to bleeding out. I managed to keep my eyes open just enough to see the two figures enter the room. I had expected to see doctors' scrubs, or nurses' uniforms, so was shocked at the sight of two bright yellow haz-mat suits.

"What's going on?" I mumbled.

"Help me get him back onto the bed," I heard one of the men say. "Then find the bloody doctor. We need him alive." I let out a yelp as they lifted me, the wound in my abdomen tearing open further. I soon heard footsteps running along the corridor outside and the man who had helped me onto the bed appeared alongside a woman, holding a clipboard. I could just about make out her face through the protective suit; pretty, maybe mid-thirties, petite. I listened as the men explained they had found me slumped against the door. They pointed out the obvious trail of blood and the doctor nodded before sending the men on their way.

"What's going on?" I asked again, my hands instinctively pressed against the opening in my guts.

"You were found at the site of the earthquake," she replied in broken English. "That was almost six months ago." My head spun with shock. I hadn't been sleeping...I'd been in a coma.

"But, this wound," I said, raising my hands a little from the area. "This wound is recent."

"We had to perform a small procedure," the doctor continued. "We had to remove something." Now she had my full attention, even in my weakened state.

"Remove what?" I asked, my voice trembling. "Like a kidney? Or my appendix? And what's with the suits?" The doctor opened one of the drawers to my left, producing a vial and a worryingly long needed.

"We need to get you fixed up. This will help with the pain, and I will get those stitches repaired. Then we will be able to tell you everything, when you are well."

Before I could protest, the needle found its way into my arm, the icy sensation of the morphine flowing through my veins rendering me unconscious in seconds.

I awoke in a panic, my first thought that months had yet again passed me by. This time, thankfully, the doctor was in the room when I came to.

"How long was I out?" I asked.

"Only a few days. We have you all fixed up, but you really must stay in bed until you have healed." I thought back to our previous conversation, what I could recall of it.

"You said you had to remove something from me?" The doctor sat on the edge of the bed with a sigh.

"You were infected with something when you were found. At first, we were treating you for a head injury, and severe dehydration. You went through some scans and we found ... an anomaly." She paused, and I could sense that she didn't want to be the one to break the news but continued regardless. "Something was growing within you."

"Like a tumour?" I asked, almost hopefully. A tumour wouldn't justify the suits, and the doctor's face gave away that it was something far worse.

"The procedure that you underwent was similar to a Caesarean section." She let that hang in the air for a moment. "Whatever *thing* you had encountered had placed something within you. We removed it, and it is being studied." Since I had awoken from the coma, I had been fixated on getting out of bed, working out why I was there. I had hardly given any thought to the earthquake but now it hit me like a slap in the face. That *thing,* the singing, the webbed hands, the darkness.

"When can I leave?" I asked, not wanting to know any more about the surgery.

"That isn't my decision, I'm afraid. This is a military laboratory and you were found to be carrying life, the sort of which we have not seen before. For the time being, the government owns you." The doctor gave me a look filled with sadness, before turning to leave and locking the door behind her. I knew then that regardless what happens with the creature they had removed from me I wouldn't be leaving that facility again.

The End

Bad Fishin'

Liam Bradley

Dennis Mann was born with fish bait in his blood. His first fishing experience-- when he was only eight, and three foot nine-- had happened at Fugini Lake, where all the beginners go. And it had treated him dandy fine.

After a long wait for a bite, his mother had suggested a little hike. Dennis stood at the water's edge, towering fishing pole in hand, eye on the bobber.

"Gee, ma," he'd whined. "The fish won't wait forever."

"You go on babe," his father had said, a humorous gleam in his dazzling blue eyes.

And so it began. After that, little Dennis Mann couldn't even go on a picnic without casting into the nearest stream. Then, one day in the dead of summer, when he was fourteen, his father announced they were going fishing at Harkness Reservoir, where the freshwater catfish lived. And it wasn't just any daytrip. It was a tradition, lived out by generations of the Mann family. Dennis caught the most catfish that day. Course, by the end of it, the teen was too weary to make the return hike, so daddy, God bless his soul (and back), carried him.

After that, Dennis never missed a year at the reservoir. Until the incident.

***

At six forty-five a.m., a four-door jeep pulled off Highway 70 and headed east on a winding dirt road. The rising sun shed fresh light onto the landscape, glimmering off metal roofs, sneaking between the red cedar trees dotting the hills ahead. Shimmering rays grasped an abandoned barn and gave its aged paint new, red life. As the jeep passed said barn, the driver, a thirty-eight-year-old Dennis Mann, reflected on the time he and his wife, Melissa, spent the night in his buddy's barn.

Never will forget that, he thought, grinning in spite of himself.

In the rear-view mirror, that barn distanced itself, as if God's hands were pulling it into eternity. Dennis looked back to the road; his expression withered with lack of sleep. He could blink away the haze in his eyes, but he couldn't shrug off the aches in his neck or the sleepiness his body clung to.

In the backseat, a rustling marked the awakening of his son Ramsey. The boy's eyes fluttered open and he stretched his limbs. But as one child awoke, the other, Lily, sagged against the window and her head lulled to the jeep's movements. With magnificent green eyes, Lily watched the hills close in on them.

Dennis positioned the mirror on her. "Tired?"

"Yeah. Never been up this early before," she replied in a drowsy voice that sucked the audio out of her tone.

Dennis nodded. "One gets used to it."

"How?"

He pursed his lips in thought. "Just does."

The road sloped downward. The red cedars followed a little further, only to have jungles of willow bushes force them back. The brush seemed to swallow them, sealing them off from civilization for good. Eventually, it became so thick that branches scraped against the jeep like monster claws. At this point, Dennis eased off the gas.

"So, how's Ram doing back there?" he asked, sounding like a sports announcer who loved their job.

"Hot," Ramsey shouted.

Dennis detected the ghost of a whine in that voice, which startled him.

"Testy, aren't we?"

With his free hand, he swiped off the heating. He then realized that he was actually sweating himself, worst of all in the armpits. Using his knee to keep the wheel leveled out, he whipped off his Yankees hoodie and laid it in the passenger seat.

Branch after branch whacked the car, bending against the windows and tires. Every other second brought with it another mighty *THWACK*.

"So, dad, are catfish hard to catch?" Lily asked.

"Oh, depends on their size. Some of them can put up a fight."

She shifted in her seat. "How big can they get?"

His eyes wandered upward as he tried to remember. "Uhhh. . .I believe the biggest on record is fifty-eight inches."

"No, I mean around here."

That gave him pause. "That I don't know. The largest one I ever caught was twenty-four."

"That had to be a battle!" Lily exclaimed, suddenly awake.

A grin split his lips. "Heck yeah, pumpkin."

Ramsey cleared his throat of gunk.

"You're first trip out here. . .were you excited?" Lily asked.

The willows at last backed off, so Dennis pressed the gas harder. "Boy was I," that mere grin became a broad smile, "I was up before six, making breakfast for myself. Grampse came out and coaxed me back to bed somehow. But I never slept again that day until I had put my worth into the sport."

"Was Grampse mad?"

Before Dennis could even process the question, Ramsey burst out, "Stop it!"

Lily tilted her head, letting hair dangle. "Stop what?"

"Asking so many questions! It's driving me flipping nuts!"

What in the hell?

"Alright!" he butted in, "relax everyone!"

"But dad, she won't shut up! What is this, a quiz?" he screamed in response.

What's gotten into him?

Dennis was prepared to ask Ramsey the very question when he felt a sharp kick against the seat. Anger stiffened him. The scowl he wore idled between concern. . .and helplessness.

Haven't heard him scream like that since he was a baby!

"Can you pull up your seat dad?" Ramsey asked. He no longer screamed, only shouted.

Dennis's foot, driven by some interpretable impulse, crushed the brake, bringing the jeep to a dirt-churning halt. Because Lily wasn't buckled in, she kissed the passenger seat.

He put on a poker face, turned 'round and faced his son, man-to-man. Ramsey wasn't pale, didn't look sick or feverish. He did have a wild glaze in his eyes that crept into Dennis like a spider.

Somewhere. . .I seen that look before. .

.

He'd hoped to intimidate, but Ramsey managed to weaken him, make him the losing party. Besides his eyes, Ramsey was the same old kid with bowl-cut hair, a clean nose, and tied shoes. At least on the outside.

"I'll pull up the seat," Dennis said in a cool manner, "*If* you ask the proper way."

Without shame, Ramsey growled, "Please."

Dennis bent over, shifted the seat about an inch forward, and then resumed his former position. Father and son locked eyes again.

"Well?"

Ramsey mumbled a lethargic "thanks".

"Good." Dennis turned to Lily and forced a smile. "Put your belt on, pumpkin."

Her seatbelt slithered around her and stiffened when she clicked it into place. Her arms trembled ever so lightly.

Dennis got the jeep rolling again. It wound around a bend, and then the hills rose higher into the sky. By this time, the sun had risen over the trees. It brightened the path which the trio traveled.

After an interlude of silence, Ramsey asked, in his recurring nasty way, "Are we close?"

"Yes. Now quiet, understand?"

No answer was sufficient enough, he supposed. Another brief silence haunted them.

"Lily? Did you have more questions?" he asked.

Lily looked up from her fingernails and took a moment to answer. "No."

"Sure? Ramsey won't interrupt again, I promise."

She shook her head. Silence clouded the remaining length of the drive.

That look. . .I've seen it before. Where, dammit?

The question haunted him. The harder he tried to get the answer, the tighter his muscles became. The answer was beyond reach. It shouldn't have been, but it was. And boy did it toy with him, as if it were a cat and he a caged canary.

The jeep passed a wooden bridge, under a grove of cottonwoods that looked awfully out of place. At last, the crooked sign greeted them from the roadside. It read:

HARKNESS RESERVOIR TRAILHEAD

Dennis parked below the trailhead itself, on the grassy roadside. He cut the engine and then chided, "Who's ready for some catfishing!"

Lily giggled. "I am!"

Every door except the driver's open from the outside. Dennis got out and opened Ramsey's door. The boy's seatbelt retracted. He hopped out and leaned against the jeep, crossing his arms. "I'm not carrying anything," he muttered.

"We'll see about that."

As he rounded the vehicle, a coldness Dennis had never experienced before seethed into his bones. Gooseflesh broke out on his skin.

Am I...scared?

The very idea made him want to laugh. Yet it didn't. He opened Lily's door. She gave him a hug. Gazing up at him, her demeanor took on the image of determination, that of a strong, mature woman, not a darling ten-year-old. Dennis predicted he would see things like that in her more and more until she became such a woman, built by inner strength and cautious maturity.

They broke up. She went to open the jeep's back.

A shrill wind blew through from the south. He shivered--yes, shivered, as if he belonged in a warmthless cave, shaking, crying out from black lungs. Shrugging the tingle off best he could, Dennis sat on the jeep's floor and began assembling fishing poles. Lily stood by, hands clasped behind her back, glancing about the area.

"Is this going to be a hard hike?" she asked.

Rubbing a halved pole against his nose, Dennis grunted. "Nah. Cousin Jeff was a year older than you when he first did it, and he came off better than me."

Lily shrugged.

Dennis fiddled with the eye of the hook. He held it near his eyes.

Contacts, the miracle of the century my ass, he thought.

"Ram," he called, "come watch." Those words, as they tumbled out, sounded foreign.

From the other side: "Why?"

"Because you need to know this stuff."

No response. No Ramsey. A tiny cloud of despair muddled Lily's princess-face. "He's acting strange dad," she whispered.

"I know." Beneath worm cans, leather-bound fly books, and tobacco cans containing lures, he found a plastic bag of hooks. "Some people have bad days."

Lily glanced to the right. "Just like mom, before they took her away."

THAT'S WHERE.

Everything clamped together like a jigsaw puzzle. Melissa, curled into the corner of a padded room...screeching like a barn owl...that evil glaze coating her eyes that had once been so beautiful, so...normal.

How did I miss it? Ramsey. . .that hateful glare. . .

Dennis froze. Nothing felt right, not the air, not his own body. The sensation

171

lasted a full minute, pouring cold sweat down his spine. Awakening fear inside him. He couldn't understand that fear, magnifying its presence.

The pole almost dropped. His mouth *did.*

Like an angel stabbing darkness, Lily said, "Last night, I had a dream you married Miranda Cosgrove."

Impossibly, he laughed. "No more iCarly for you."

"In the dream, you had to teach Miranda how to boil eggs because she'd never learned."

More laughter. Impossible, redeeming laughter. "That's pretty bad. Course, there's probably people out there who can't even boil water, much less eggs."

"What's the strangest dream you ever had?"

Dennis finished his pole and began working on Ramsey's.

"Lessee. Once I dreamed I won a Coca-Cola bike in a gas station contest."

"Was the station real?"

He paused. "No, don't think it was."

Lily resumed glancing around. On the other side, Ramsey spat in the dirt.

"Dad, are you going to remarry?"

Back into the abyss he fell. Wherever the question had come from, Dennis didn't care to venture. He set aside his patient and leaned forward. "Certainly not. I love your mother far too much to do that."

The dullness he spoke with pressed him to wonder whether or not he told the truth.

"But you're divorced. She's gone. There's no going back," Lily said.

"Hey, the only reason we're divorced is because mommy's sick. Her mental health is a very hard thing to live with, with her medical bills and all her suffering. But, if the doctors can fix her up this summer, I'm going to re-marry her."

Lily's face lit up like a beacon for lost souls. That magical determination reclaimed her stature.

"Really?" she asked, unbelieving.

"Oh sure. So don't worry."

She nodded.

He collected his creel, backpack, and water bottle, which he clipped to his jeans. Lily got the honor of transporting a covered bucket of chicken livers. She made a face as she took them.

"Ram, come get your water," Dennis demanded.

The boy strode out into the road. Dennis tossed him the bottle. He caught it with one hand.

"Whoa! Nice!" Lily exclaimed. "How'd you do that?"

Amazed, Dennis would've been . . . if not for that creeping cold . . . the wind was still there but it couldn't have been, it died minutes ago . . .

In a flash of movement, Ramsey darted onto the trail and took off running, forcing them to begin the trek.

***

Ramsey hit the hillside and its steep incline slowed his mad dash. The others caught up, each short of breath.

"Hold up! I need water!" Lily pleaded.

The boy kept struggling.

"Ram! Stop!"

Lily inhaled gulps of water. Some spilled on her chin. After she came up for air, Dennis wiped it away with his palm.

Some deep breaths later, she said, "Okay, let's go."

Ramsey started up the hill again. As he followed behind, Dennis watched the boy's tennis shoes slide precariously in the loose dirt.

Trees shaded their hike to the top. Despite the umbrella of limbs, Dennis didn't feel so cold now. However, he *did* feel wasted, as if he'd spent the morning pushing boulders around. The fishing gear didn't help. He couldn't complain too much, as, up ahead, the trail headed downhill.

Ramsey's flashing movements never evaded Dennis's attention. They reminded him of today's troubles. Reminded him: *something's wrong. Something's not right.*

The trail twisted sharply at various points, sometimes pointing up, sometimes straight. Twenty minutes later, the land flattened out. Lily passed her father, the bucket swinging in her hand, her backpack bouncing like a potbelly. The trail fed into a valley where hills sloped up on each side. Somewhere along the way, Lily said over her shoulder, "You know dad, I really think I belong in the wilderness. Like, mother nature made me special, to live with her. I've always wanted a cabin out in the forest."

Dennis snorted. The sound wasn't exactly pleasant, but it was sincere.

"What?"

"Oh, I used to want the same thing," he explained. "I still do."

"Yeah?"

"Mmhmm."

Lily spun around and began walking backwards. Her hands clutched the backpack's shoulder straps.

"So, is the reservoir close?" she asked.

He nodded. "Now watch it. You might trip."

The valley became a small canyon. They stopped there for water and to let Lily investigate the smooth rock walls. After that, the trail picked up and stretched over two more hills. Atop the second, they peered down at the first big pond. Ramsey actually stood beside them, seeming at peace. Dennis took Lily up on his shoulder and pointed. Perched in a tree four yards away were two golden eagles.

"Wow! Is that rare?" Lily asked.

Dennis met her gaze. He shared her smile. "Yep. Beautiful creatures."

He reached out to pull Ramsey close, but the boy shook off his hand and ran into the trees.

"Be careful!"

They made their way down. Dozens of willow bushes stood between them and the pond. Ever cautious, they pushed through. Ramsey came upon the pond's sandy shores first. When Dennis and Lily emerged, he shied back several steps, almost sinking right back into the jungle.

"Okay, tick check!" Dennis said.

His fingers turned back Lily's ears, picked through her hair, checked her belly button. Lily then wandered to the water's edge.

Dennis turned to his son. "Your turn, Ram."

The boy retreated another step. A sigh--held back in hope, forced down by ignorance--escaped Dennis. He glanced along the ground.

"Something's wrong, Ramsey," he said at last.

The boy made no effort to reply or move.

"What is it?" Dennis asked. He stood erect and took a few steps forward. Ramsey, by some miracle, remained.

"Seriously, what's the problem?"

He knew. Yet he ventured a few more steps. Ramsey didn't flee.

An honest sorrow consumed Dennis's eyes. "Was it talking about mom? I shouldn't do that around you."

Wind whirled, chipping the pond's crystal surface. As it blew past him, Dennis heard--would've sworn, would've died to prove it--bells jangling. The sound even echoed after it was gone, once. A bubble of time existed when Dennis didn't belong in his surroundings. But once the wind died, the bubble popped. An eerie silence dominated the following seconds until it wasn't silence anymore, but a growing buzz in Dennis's ear. It got louder, louder. . . louder. . .

Dennis clapped his hands.

"How 'bout some lunch?" he asked no one in particular.

"No thanks," Lily said. "I'm gonna fish first."

Ramsey continued to stare.

"Well, I'm hungry. I'm gonna eat," Dennis said. He collected Lily's backpack, sat on his bum, and dug for a shrink-wrapped ham sandwich.

"Dad?" Lily's voice came to him from somewhere close. He looked up. "Please, could you bait the hook? Won't take long."

"Sure."

Lily held her nose and watched as Dennis slipped dark red meat chunks onto the hook. He could feel Ramsey's gaze wrapping around him like a tarp.

I can't even look my boy in the eye, he thought. A queasiness burned in his stomach. Never had the stench of chicken livers made him nauseous, like it did now.

"There," he grunted, handing Lily the pole. An excited fire blazed in her eyes.

Dennis headed for the backpack. He didn't know if he even could eat now, but the hole in his innards demanded filling. Plus, the last thing he'd eaten that morning was a slice of cheese, and it had left a strange, bitter aftertaste in his mouth.

Halfway to the pack, he halted.

Ramsey was gone. Dennis's eyes swept the willows, the shore, found nothing. Already, sweat beads dampened his forehead.

Don't panic. Maybe he went to take a leak. God let it be that.

He turned back to Lily. The girl was reeling back, preparing for a winner cast. . .the hook soared, plunked beneath the surface. She reeled in steadily while giving the catfish plenty of time to smell and taste, and, she hoped, bite.

"Stay here pumpkin, Ramsey's gone. I'm gonna look for 'im," he said.

She nodded. Not even for such a startling message did she avert her eyes from that rolling line.

Dennis let the jungle swallow him. Struggling through poky brush, he came upon a place where the willows stood back to watch the sunlight bathe the sand.

"Ramsey?" Dennis called.

He expected silence. Instead, the wind blew. Rustled the willows, giving them the image of angered gods. The bells jangled again, this time in a rhythm, playing an ominous tune.

"Ram! Answer me!" he shouted, trying to drown the bells. "Ram! Ram!"

He spun in a circle, unsure of which direction to take. At length, he settled on going forward. He struggled to cover ground, spending too much time shoving aside branches. All the while calling, "Ramsey! Ram! Ram! RAMSEY!!!"

Those hellish bells followed him wherever he searched, jangling various tunes toned to insidious frequencies. The wind chose to remain at a steady breeze, frigid enough to chill Dennis right through the skin.

At one point, he paused, cupped his mouth and screamed, "Ramsey, damn brat, answer me!"

Then he gasped. Shock muted him. Unhealthy bouts of fear numbed his legs. He'd never sworn before, not in the children's presence. Not even in Melissa's presence. Sure, he'd thought many a' nasty thought, but for hell's sake didn't we all at some point?

Before Dennis could recover, a vision materialized over the surrounding world. A vision of Melissa herself, on a hospital bed, where she had passed so many ragged days, fighting off more than one illness but unaware of it. Each had infected Dennis too, but in a different way, one which every caring husband knew to one degree or another.

With each rise and fall of Melissa's chest, the bells rose an octave. They headed for a climax, playing tune after tune, each portraying the very sounds of unbearable loneliness. Then, a wild shriek overpowered them. Melissa shattered into pieces and darkness remained. Dennis opened his eyes, which felt heavy, as if fresh from a peaceful sleep.

Pinpointing the noise, he dashed into the willows, fought to reach his boy. A branch tore a strip of cloth from his shirt on the way. Ramsey stood before another pond. This one couldn't have been more than eight yards wide, eleven long, and was shrouded by a few cottonwoods. Ramsey clutched the bucket in one hand.

Dennis breathed a relieved sigh, along with jumbled words that eased some of the tension gripping him.

Ramsey turned around. The wind, bells, and coldness, all returned with a vengeance. Neither man moved, as if time held them in place. At length, Ramsey lifted the bucket. Gradually, it rose above his head. . . it tilted . . . livers rained over him like pieces of a meteor. Sticky red goo matted the boy's hair.

Another shriek. Ramsey whirled, ran. Dove into the water. Vanished. A blurred interlude came next. Dennis never remembered it. The next thing he saw-- through water-logged eyes--was Ramsey lying on the sand. Dennis breathed life into him. Again. Again. Again. But the life wouldn't stay. Hope slipped away like dusk. Dennis sobbed harder than he'd ever before.

"No," an unsteady voice broke the quiet. Lily crawled over. He enfolded his petrified little angel in his arms. Held her. Held her oh so tight.

***

The jeep traveled beneath a colorful sky. Orange-purple hues swirled against a crystal backdrop, where the sun once hung, providing what little comfort it could. The trees now towered like black, faceless giants employed to guard the critter world below.

In the jeep, behind Lily, the body rested, wrapped in bent willow rods. Lily kept glancing at it. Perhaps she hoped signs of life might've stuck around and were working to revive young Ramsey. When Dennis caught glimpses of those princess eyes, he saw nothingness, which only increased the urge to hug her again.

Bells of a different sort played, as if someone inside Dennis's head was beating up and down a xylophone. Between beats, words huffed.

Melissa. . . . . . . .Melissa. . . .I'm. . . . . . .sorry darling. . . . .

The End

Sinkhole

Dale Parnell

Kieran woke up. Not a slow, groggy, still half asleep awake, but a sudden, 'someone flicked a switch' awake.

He lay perfectly still beneath the duvet, every nerve in his body tense and on edge. His first thought was that someone was in the house, that his sleeping brain had heard a noise and had flooded his system with adrenaline, getting him ready to fight. He carefully reached a hand out across the mattress, his fingertips brushing Zoe's back, and she murmured briefly before falling silent again.

Kieran eased his body out from underneath the duvet, careful not to disturb Zoe. She was due to hear about the promotion tomorrow and it had taken her ages to fall asleep, the anxiety and anticipation of the announcement keeping her mind ticking over far too late. He lifted himself off the bed and stood for a moment, head tilted, mouth open, straining to listen.

There didn't appear to be anything, certainly nothing he could hear now. Ordinarily he would have gotten back in bed and gone back to sleep, but he felt so wide awake that he knew there was little point.

Gingerly he slipped out of the bedroom and padded downstairs.

The clock in the kitchen told him it was just after three in the morning. Kieran did a quick check of the doors and windows; everything was shut tight. Some people liked to sleep with a window open, letting the cool night air circulate around the house. Kieran wasn't one of those people. Doors and windows were for the daytime, for letting sunshine and warm air into your home. At night they became a barricade, a padlock to be closed and locked to keep everything you held dear safe and secure.

Kieran filled a glass from the kitchen tap and stood staring at his dim reflection in the kitchen window. He was twenty-nine, three weeks away from thirty, working in a job he was good at, with a house that was twenty-five years away from being his. He and Zoe had been seeing each other for six years. They'd get married in two or three years and start a family.

This was his life, he told himself. This was his life and it was a good one.

As his eyes grew accustomed to the dark, Kieran noticed something out in the back garden, beyond his own reflection. About three quarters down the length of the garden was an overgrown laurel bush that Kieran had been planning to remove ever since he moved into the house. It cast a huge shadow over the bottom of the garden and took up far too much space.

Standing on the cold tiled floor of his kitchen at three seventeen in the morning, Kieran suddenly realised that the laurel was gone.

It was cold outside, colder than Kieran would have thought for August, no matter what time it was, and he pulled his thin jacket tightly around his body, the frigid air stinging his bare legs. His feet were rubbing inside his trainers, but he ignored the discomfort and edged further out across the patio, the light from his mobile phone screen barely reaching further than a few inches in front of him. The back garden was about forty feet long. The first ten feet was patio, the rest was taken up with a tired lawn, with flower beds running along the borders. As Kieran stepped off the edge of the patio onto the grass, he saw it, although he couldn't believe it. Where the bottom third of his back garden had been, there was nothing. The ground had literally opened up and swallowed everything. Kieran had heard about sinkholes, but he had always assumed they happened over old coal mines, and this area had never been mined. Kieran shuffled towards the lip of the hole, soil and stones breaking away from the ragged edge and tumbling silently down into the void. Kieran held his mobile out nervously, as if fearful that an unseen hand was going to leap up and snatch it out his hand at any moment. The hole looked to be about ten feet across, almost a perfect circle, and in this light it was impossible to gauge how deep it went. Kieran scanned the ground, and bending down carefully he dislodged a fist-sized clump of earth from the edge of the hole. Stretching his arm out he dropped it, waiting to hear the soft thump as it hit the bottom.

Nothing.

Kieran stood waiting, listening, staring down into the hole. And for one brief moment, it happened. It was like being suddenly blind and deaf, but not really because you knew you could see and hear, it was just that there was nothing to be seen, and nothing to be heard. There was nothing down there, and the nothing of it was spilling up and out from the centre of the world and it would cover the earth and there would be nothing ever again.

Kieran's legs buckled, and for one terrifying moment he thought he was going to pitch forward into the hole, and the thought of falling down there made him feel so sick and afraid and small that Kieran let out a high pitched, childlike cry that seemed to fill the world, until there was only his fear and the hole left.

Kieran fell backwards onto the lawn, his fingers clawing down into the grass, rooting him to the spot, fists clenching and holding on, his eyes still locked on the hole at his feet. From behind him Kieran heard the patio door slide open and Zoe's voice was calling his name.

"...ran. Kieran. What are you doing? You're going to be late."

Gradually the sound of birds singing drifted down to him, cars running along the main road at the end of their street, the wind stirring tree branches and the loose fence panels in their neighbour's garden. But most surprisingly, Kieran realised it was light.

"What the bloody hell is that?" asked Zoe, suddenly standing beside Kieran, holding a cup of tea in front of his face.

"It's a hole," replied Kieran, his hand lifting up to take the mug.

"I can see it's a hole, how did it get here?" replied Zoe dryly.

"I don't know."

***

The ground surveyor stood in Kieran's back garden; pen poised over his clipboard. Kieran could understand the hi-vis jacket, maybe it was his work coat, but the hard hat seemed a step too far. The hole was in the ground – what exactly did the guy think was going to hit him on the head?

"And you say this just appeared overnight?"

"Yes," replied Kieran, keeping his eyes on the surveyor.

"Hmmm."

The surveyor made a note on his clipboard and then pulled a tape measure from his coat pocket. Setting the clipboard down on the grass he proceeded to take some measurements, running the stiff metal tape across the mouth of the hole in a few places, before standing at the edge and running the tape straight downwards. Kieran waited as the surveyor fed the tape down into the earth.

"Huh," sounded the surveyor eventually.

"What's wrong?" asked Kieran.

"We'll need to come back to take some readings. I don't think I can reach the bottom with this."

"Okay," replied Kieran, casting a brief glance at the hole, the first time he had looked at it again since the surveyor had arrived that morning. "How deep do you think it could be?"

"It's difficult to tell. But it's definitely deeper than ten metres," he replied, chuckling to himself.

Kieran took a step backwards towards the house.

"Is it safe?" he asked.

The surveyor looked up and down the garden a few times, seemingly weighing things up in his head.

"Yeah, should be," he replied, unconvincingly. "But if the hole gets any wider, you may want to find somewhere else to sleep for the night. Just in case."

Kieran showed the surveyor back through the house. Handing over his business card, the surveyor promised he would call later that afternoon to book a time for the inspection team to call round. Kieran called his line manager at work and explained the situation. Claudia agreed that given the situation it would be best if Kieran worked from home whilst he waited for the inspection team to declare everything safe. Kieran called Zoe at work but got her answerphone. He'd forgotten she was supposed to hear about the promotion today and he ended up leaving a garbled message that he was sure didn't make sense. He pulled himself together enough at the end of the message to wish her luck.

He made himself some lunch, but picked at it, not really feeling hungry, and every so often caught himself staring out of the kitchen window down the back garden. He tried getting some work done but he couldn't concentrate, he was struggling to answer simple emails. He couldn't shake the worry that the hole was getting bigger, that it would open up wider and wider until it damaged the house, or worse.

Standing by the window in their back bedroom, Kieran stared down at the hole. Even in bright daylight the hole seemed impossibly dark, as if it was emitting the darkness, like some kind of reverse light. Tearing his eyes away from the hole, Kieran spied the dilapidated shed that was struggling to stand up at the very bottom of the garden. Like the overgrown laurel bush, this was a remnant from the previous owner, and Kieran had poked his head through the door a handful of times before deciding that he would eventually knock it down, maybe putting up a small sheltered bench to catch the last of the afternoon sunshine. Looking at it now, something tickled at the back of Kieran's mind, something he had seen in the shed, something useful. The previous owner had been a much keener gardener than Kieran and there were signs that they had grown their own vegetables over the years, including climbing beans. Tucked up in one corner of the old shed there was a bundle of bamboo sticks. And Kieran knew exactly what he was going to do with them.

Being this close to the edge of the hole made Kieran feel sick, and he was sweating much more than he would have liked to admit. But it was important. He needed to see if the hole got any bigger.

Getting as close as he dared, Kieran carefully pushed the bamboo sticks into the ground around the edge of the hole. Zoe had gone through a phase of knitting a year or two back, resulting in a total of two and half scarves. But she still had a dozen or so balls of yarn left over. Kieran chose a bright orange, something that would stand out, and once all the sticks were in place, he carefully wound the wool around the sticks, tying it loosely in place. Kieran backed away from the hole, wiping his hands roughly across his face and trying to bring his breathing back down to normal. But it was done. If the hole got any bigger, the sticks would topple, and he would instantly know something was wrong.

When Zoe got back from work, he showed her his handiwork from the kitchen window. She laughed at first, but then seeing Kieran's face she hugged him and agreed that it was a good idea.

"Anyway," she added, "aren't you going to ask me?"

Kieran looked at her blankly for a moment before finally realising what she was talking about.

"Oh god, of course! Well, did you get it?"

"Did I get what?" asked Zoe, grinning smugly.

"The promotion, smart-arse, did you get it?" replied Kieran.

"That's Department Manager Smart-Arse, I'll have you know!"

"I knew you'd get it," beamed Kieran, scooping her up and hugging her fiercely. He stood holding her, enjoying the feeling of her arms around his neck.

"At least we can afford to deal with that now, whatever it is," said Zoe, looking out of the window at Kieran's impromptu safety barrier.

"Yes," replied Kieran, letting Zoe slip down onto the floor again.

"Meena says I can start straight away; they just need to get my office sorted out. Margaret won't be leaving until the end of the month obviously, but Meena says she wants me ready to pick up the slack as soon as, make sure there's no break in service, you know. Oh, and I spoke to Rob and Sanj at lunch time, did you know...."

Zoe carried on talking, oblivious to the fact that Kieran was no longer listening, not really. He nodded and smiled in the right places, but throughout it all he kept his gaze on the thin orange line that was flickering slightly in the breeze, waiting for something to happen.

***

It was another two days before the inspection team came out. The surveyor had called and apologised, saying that there was a shortage of appointments over the summer months, but insisting that Kieran should call him if anything changed. After seeing Zoe off to work, Kieran waited in the living room, ignoring the television in the corner, until the doorbell rang. The surveyor smiled, shook his hand, and introduced him to the small team of three very young-looking inspectors. They all had bright yellow hi-vis jackets and hard hats on and were laden down with large holdalls jammed full of measuring equipment. Kieran showed them through the house to the back garden.

"Did you do that?" asked the surveyor, indicating the bamboo sticks and orange wool.

"Yeah," replied Kieran rather sheepishly.

"Nice," said the surveyor. "Obviously we'll have to take it down whilst we work, but I might borrow that myself for the future."

After giving the inspection team their instructions, they got to work unpacking their equipment and lifting the bamboo sticks up out of the ground. Kieran watched as one of the team lay down on her stomach and edged towards the lip of the hole, pointing a camera over the edge and taking a few pictures, each click of the camera shutter accompanied by a bright flash of white light. Seeing the girl that close to the edge of the hole was turning Kieran's stomach, so he turned and went back to house. The surveyor called out that they would be about two hours, and Kieran waved a hand over his head, not wanting to look back to the hole, or what the team were doing.

True to his word, just over two hours later the surveyor knocked on the back door. Kieran had managed to get some work done, but not much. Every time he heard a noise or voice from the back garden he panicked that something terrible had happened, and he began to picture himself repelling down a rope into the hole, the black emptiness of it swallowing him whole, the open mouth of the hole getting further and further away, smaller and smaller, until it was gone altogether, and he was alone in the pitch black, at the end of a rope that he knew couldn't hold his weight forever, waiting for it to snap and send him hurtling downwards, into oblivion.

Stepping in the back garden, Kieran could see that the other team had already packed up, and he showed them through the house to their vans. The surveyor said he had some paperwork to finalise for Kieran to sign, and that he would help him put the bamboo sticks back in place.

Walking around the edge of the hole, the surveyor had replaced four of the sticks before Kieran had planted one.

"It's okay, you get used to working around all sorts of things in my job," said the surveyor, indicating that he would finish the rest. Kieran took a step back, hands in his pockets, feeling slightly emasculated as the surveyor casually plodded around the circumference of the hole, pushing the sticks firmly into the ground.

"Do you know what caused it?" asked Kieran, trying to distract himself from feeling like a coward.

"Well that's the interesting thing," smiled the surveyor, "there's no record of any sinkholes in this area before now, not for hundreds of miles. There're no mines of any sort, and no natural geological features that we've been able to identify. It could be underground water, or maybe a pocket of natural gas that ignited, but you would have heard that a few streets over, and there would be a blast radius of debris. It's a brain teaser, that's for sure."

"Is it safe though?" asked Kieran, nervously taking a step closer, determined to ignore the knot in his stomach.

"As best we can tell, this is as big as it's going to get. We've taken samples from all over the garden, down a few metres, and the ground seems solid enough."

The surveyor was stood on the far side of the hole facing Kieran, the last of the bamboo sticks held in his hands, ready to push into the soil.

"It's just one of those freak incidents, Mr. Corveign, no way to predict them, no way to prevent them." The surveyor beamed a smile at Kieran, and then pushed the last stick down into the soil between his feet.

And Kieran knew. It was like before, when the void of the sinkhole seemed to stretch up into the world and smother everything with... nothing. There was no sound, no light. There was just that look on the surveyor's face as he finally understood it himself... before the ground at his feet crumbled away to nothing and he fell. Kieran expected to hear a scream, but there was nothing.

Nothing at all.

***

"How did it go today?"

"Sorry? asked Kieran.

"Today, with the inspection people? Did they say what's happening out there?" Zoe was sat at their dining table and Kieran was placing a plate of chicken and pasta salad down in front of her, a second plate in his other hand.

Kieran didn't know how long Zoe had been home. He didn't remember her coming back, he didn't remember cooking dinner. He realised, with a cold, hard feeling spreading through his gut, that he couldn't remember anything since the surveyor had fallen.

"Oh, it was fine," replied Kieran, sitting down next to her. "They say it's fine, nothing to worry about."

***

It was six days before someone from the ground surveyors team tried calling Kieran. For the first two or three times he let the calls go to answerphone, but the messages were getting more concerning - the surveyor hadn't been heard from since leaving Kieran's house, and did Kieran have any idea about where he was going that evening? On the third message the surveyor's assistant mentioned the police, and so the next time they called Kieran answered. He told the assistant that the surveyor had been finishing up his paperwork but had received a phone call and had left suddenly. No, Kieran hadn't heard from him again. And yes, the sinkhole was still in his garden and he had no idea what to do about it. In the end, the assistant apologised to Kieran for the department leaving him in the lurch and promised that someone would be round to discuss what steps could be taken with regards to fixing the problem.

The next day a very officious looking woman in a dark grey suit arrived at the house. She introduced herself as Julia and apologised for the delay, explaining that the inspection team hadn't been able to verify the exact depth of the sinkhole, and so it was going to be difficult to offer any solutions regarding filling the hole in.

"So what does that mean?" asked Kieran.

"It means that until we can confirm the extent of the void we are dealing with, we are really only left with one option, which is to cap the mouth of the hole."

"You mean put a lid on it?" asked Kieran, slightly alarmed at the seemingly low-tech solution that he was being offered.

"It would be a temporary solution Mr. Corveign, just to make it safe whilst we continue the investigation."

"What are we talking about, a few planks of wood?"

"No," laughed Julia, "we'd be installing a sheet of reinforced steel that is securely riveted to the ground. One of the things I need to do today is verify that there hasn't been any change in the diameter of the sinkhole so that we can have the correct size manufactured."

Kieran felt his skin prickle cold with sweat. He hadn't been out into the back garden since that day, and he had made sure Zoe didn't go out there either, saying that he wanted to wait to hear back that the area was safe.

"Do you mind if I take just a quick look?" asked Julia.

"Is it safe to do so, I mean, shouldn't we just stay away from it?" asked Kieran, feeling his shirt sticking to his back.

"I'm afraid we can't just ignore it, Mr. Corveign. Trust me, I'll be very careful, and it won't take a moment."

Before Kieran could argue, Julia had stood up and was retrieving a camera and measuring tape from her bag. She stood patiently, waiting for Kieran to show her to the back garden. His mind was racing, desperate to think of some reason why they shouldn't go out there. He couldn't go back out there, not again.

"I'm sorry to rush you Mr. Corveign but I do need to get these measurements back to the office as soon as possible, we need to make sure that the area is made safe as soon as we can."

Kieran pushed himself up from the sofa slowly. There was nothing he could say now that wouldn't look suspicious. Zoe had already started to question why it was taking them so long to fix the problem. If he ignored it any longer, she would end up calling the council herself, and then it would be out of his hands.

"Of course," said Kieran eventually, "this way."

***

"Did Will put these here?" asked Julia, pointing to the bamboo sticks that encircled the mouth of the sinkhole.

"Umm, yes," replied Kieran.

"Strange, it isn't typical procedure."

Julia edged towards the mouth of the hole, moving much more cautiously than the surveyor had done. She clicked a few photographs and then took a couple of measurements across the mouth of the hole, noting a few numbers down on her own clipboard.

"Has the edge always been like this?" asked Julia. Kieran looked up to see that she was stood on the other side of the hole, a metre or so away from the spot where the surveyor had fallen. The edge of the hole was irregular here, looking like an extra bite had been taken out of the side.

"Yes, I believe so," said Kieran, feeling his skin prickle hot.

"Strange that Will didn't mark around this section," muttered Julia, casting her gaze around the edge of the hole, noting the regular placement of the bamboo sticks.

"Maybe he ran out of sticks," said Kieran, who had suddenly appeared beside Julia, causing her to flinch ever so slightly.

"Well, there are some more just there," said Julia, pointing to the side of the shed where a few more of the bamboo sticks stood leaning against the shed door.

"Maybe he got scared," said Kieran.

Julia turned back to Kieran, who was now stood at the edge of the hole, staring down into it, his shoulders limp, arms hanging at his sides.

"Mr. Corveign, maybe you should move away from the edge please?" said Julia, unsure if the crack in her voice was panic or fear.

"Do you think it wants to be filled up again?" said Kieran, his voice barely a whisper.

"Mr. Corveign, please, I don't think it's safe to be that close." She edged closer to Kieran, arms held out in front of her, wondering if she would be able to pull him back away from the hole. Julia slid one foot across the grass, her fingertips just grazing Kieran's shirt, ready to grab hold when suddenly Kieran spun around and snatched her wrists in his hands. She yelled in surprise, trying but failing to wriggle out of his grip.

"I think it does," said Kieran, his unblinking eyes staring into Julia's.

He knew, and now so did the woman, just as the surveyor had known. As he tensed his arms and lifted upwards, he could see that the woman understood. He watched as she tried to scream but realised that no sound was coming out. She tried to see, but there was no light to see by. It had been taken, swallowed whole by the void, by the nothing that lived deep underground. People said that the heart of the world was a burning maelstrom, but it's not. It's cold and it's dark and there's nothing at all. That's why Kieran had to fill it. He had to fill it with something. He let go of the woman's wrists and watched her fall into the black, empty void. She wouldn't be enough, not nearly enough.

But it didn't matter.

Kieran could fix that.

The End

Printed in Poland
by Amazon Fulfillment
Poland Sp. z o.o., Wrocław